"What is all this?"

"Payment for the free dinner yesterday," Buck said easily. "The coil for your hot-water heater. A gasket for the faucet, and a fuse for the burner on the stove. Now will you let me in so I can install them?"

Loren flushed. "That's very nice, but no thank you," she said firmly.

"You're not going to stand there and deny you need a man around here."

She glared at him furiously. She knew what he had come back for, and it wasn't plumbing. She wasn't denying that she'd responded to him like some wanton little . . . whatever. Which was just the point. She needed no further complications in her life. "Just go away, Buck," she said in a low voice.

With a wicked glint in his eye, he said, "I don't think so."

Dear Reader:

Three months ago we were delighted to announce the arrival of TO HAVE AND TO HOLD, the thrilling new romance series that takes you into the world of married love. We're pleased to report that letters of praise and enthusiasm are pouring in daily. TO HAVE AND TO HOLD is clearly off to a great start!

TO HAVE AND TO HOLD is the first and only series that portrays the joys and heartaches of marriage. Its unique concept makes it significantly different from the other lines now available to you, and it presents stories that meet the high standards set by SECOND CHANCE AT LOVE. TO HAVE AND TO HOLD offers all the compelling romance, exciting sensuality, and heartwarming entertainment you expect.

We think you'll love TO HAVE AND TO HOLD—and that you'll become the kind of loyal reader who is making SECOND CHANCE AT LOVE an ever-increasing success. Read about love affairs that last a lifetime. Look for three TO HAVE AND TO HOLD romances each and every month, as well as six SECOND CHANCE AT LOVE romances each month. We hope you'll read and enjoy them all. And please keep writing! Your thoughts about our books are very important to us.

Warm wishes,

Ellen Edwards

Ellen Edwards
SECOND CHANCE AT LOVE
The Berkley Publishing Group
200 Madison Avenue
New York, N.Y. 10016

Second Chance at Love

KISSES FROM HEAVEN

JEANNE GRANT

A
SECOND CHANCE AT LOVE
BOOK

Other Second Chance at Love books by
Jeanne Grant

MAN FROM TENNESSEE   #119
A DARING PROPOSITION   #149

KISSES FROM HEAVEN

KISSES
FROM HEAVEN

Chapter

1

"LOREN!"

Loren Shephard backed up four steps with a dozen folders in her hands, not to mention a coffee cup, legal pad, and, dangling precariously from her little finger, a pair of tortoise-shell safety glasses. "I've been trying to avoid you all morning," she said candidly to the heavily jowled man behind the streamlined teak desk.

Her boss raised a severe eyebrow that would have quelled half the employees in the plant and sighed at Loren's total lack of response. "The day I fire you I'm going to have to put on a pair of running shoes just to catch up with you," he told her. "Don't you *ever* just sit at your desk and hide behind a newspaper like everyone else who works here?"

"Like you, sweetheart?"

"Sit down and behave yourself."

She complied, perching on the arm of one of Frank's massive office chairs. Her soft, teasing smile faded as she juggled the paraphernalia she was carrying in order to lower the glasses onto the end of her nose. As a businesslike

1

gesture, it lacked something, probably because it was close to impossible for a scant hundred pounds of redhead with big gray eyes to radiate the aura of a female executive. She'd stopped worrying about that; she and Frank had resolved the women's competence issue a long time ago.

At the moment, her slim leg was still swinging impatiently; she had a hectic schedule this Friday and had no time to waste chatting up the boss. Frank acknowledged her body language with a grimace of recognition. For the last four years, he had been alternately fascinated by the shape of that swinging leg and irritated all out of proportion that his one female manager was more interested in her job than in currying favor with him.

"Accounting sent down paper work for six raises," he said gruffly, tossing her a clipped set of papers that she recognized as having originated with her office. "Dammit, Loren, you know what economic conditions are, and I expressly told everyone at the last staff meeting that there would be no raises for anyone until further notice."

"Yes," she agreed, "but then there's the difference between the letter and the spirit of the law, Frank. A few selective raises don't affect the balance sheets, and when the economy *does* improve, you have to have men in the plant who know what they're doing. These particular electricians are too damned good to lose—and they know they can get jobs anywhere, regardless of the economy." She added, very gently, "We've been through this before."

Frank's thick, beefy hand smoothed back the nonexistent hair on his bald scalp. "That's no excuse for going over my head."

"I didn't go over your head, Frank," Loren said wryly. "I told you I was going to do it last week." She paused. "Did you sign them?"

His glare confirmed her minor victory. "Besides, there's a morale problem when you give out raises to only a few—"

She shook her head. "Just the opposite. Your salesmen and engineers can be replaced a dime a dozen, Frank. But the production people—the ones who make *you* money—

are going to know you're thinking of the plant people first, not the ivory-tower snobs in the office."

He leaned forward, making an elaborate show of shuffling papers on his desk. "Just don't do it again."

"Yes, Frank." She stood up.

"And don't go using that 'snob' lingo in the offices."

"Yes, Frank."

"And I'd like to see you give me just *half* the loyalty you give the plant workers," he barked gruffly.

"Yes, Frank."

"Shut up, Loren."

She gave him a cheeky grin and perched the glasses on top of her rusty curls, gathering the folders back together in her arms.

"One other thing . . ."

She half-turned in the doorway, a question in her eyes at Frank's oddly uncomfortable tone.

"You know Matt Roberts is leaving on vacation next Friday. You can handle both personnel and production for a couple of weeks?"

What would happen, Loren wondered idly, if she told him no? Already, she packed her own job and half of his into a forty-hour week. There wasn't a day she didn't go home dead on her feet, and the Lord knew she had her own troubles. Still, so did Frank Humphreys. So did her 412 "boys," as Frank referred to the plant employees. She loved her job, and more important, the hectic hours of her work week offered complete oblivion from the hassles of her private life.

"Of course I can handle it, Frank," she assured him. "Don't worry about it."

"I wasn't worrying. I knew I could count on you, sweetheart."

Vaguely, she considered pouring her cooled cup of coffee on his head. Her annoyance was not so much for his patronizing tone as for his pat assumption—shared by all too many people lately—that she had an endless list of solutions for whatever problems might arise. She hadn't. She also didn't have the time to argue. There was an unemployment hearing at ten, then a meeting with Matt Roberts, four potential press operators to be interviewed, an insurance review...

It was two o'clock before Loren was able to call home, a sandwich in her hand and the call made standing. Her sister, Angela, had promised to watch their grandfather today. Angie was a very lush eighteen and Loren's diametric opposite in every way... particularly in the reliability department. Still, Angela had promised. The phone rang. And rang. Finally, Loren heard the receiver picked up on the other end.

"David?" whispered the sweet, silky voice.

Loren's eyes closed like shutters. "No. It's Loren. Angela, you haven't been asleep! At this hour!"

"I was out late last night..."

"Look for Gramps," Loren clipped out curtly.

Angela did not return to the phone for a full five minutes. "Look, Loren, we both know he belongs in an institution—"

Loren slammed down the receiver, her stomach feeling as if she had just swallowed barbed wire. Not again. Not another Friday afternoon like all the others... She took a breath, and then another.

A moment later, she dialed Frank, told him she was leaving, listened to his token protests, and lingered ridiculously long over putting on her coat and organizing her desk. The ache of weariness was already making itself felt in her spine, her calves, her eyes. It had been a very long week, and though Loren considered depression an unforgivable waste of time, there were occasional moments when she had to admit she had too much on her plate to handle. The house and her job, Gramps and his benders, the nubile Angela....

She applied lipstick and ran a brush quickly through her hair before leaving. Confidence builders. In the mirror, a wisp of a redhead stared back at her with dark pewter eyes, her white wool coat not unlike the cool white porclein of her complexion. Loren knew color would return in a moment. Her chin was already tilted up, and her shoulders were squared. She had more steel in her makeup than her appearance showed. The men called her "sprite" behind her back and "sexy" to her face. She dressed in feminine styles and pastel colors for them; today, a powder-blue wool sweater and matching skirt that softened her thin frame. Loren enjoyed the nicknames because she knew they were intended affectionately; more than that, she knew that she had the men's respect. There had never been a hint of an unwanted pass.

It was frigidly nasty outside. The remnants of February slush, a March wind, and a threat of snow held over from January. Her sandaled heels obstinately crisscrossed the puddles. She refused to be 5'1" unless she was prone and alone. Hugging her coat close to her, she huddled in the five-year-old van and coaxed the engine, trying to persuade the reluctant motor that it was a nice spring day and worth starting for. It vroomed finally, and Loren set off. She took Route 275 to the I-94 exit to Livernois, trying to ignore the little ball of panic in her stomach. The bar was *not* nice. The area was worse. But the sheer pity she felt for her grandfather overrode her hesitations. He had lost everything—son and daughter-in-law, wife and fortune. All too empathetically, Loren understood not only why Gramps drank but also why he insisted on doing it in a skid-row bar. *Never* an institution, she thought furiously.

A horn blared as she inadvertently weaved out of her lane. The Motor City had no tolerance for poor drivers. Which she was. Detroit liked sassy cars for that matter, and her van was close to an anachronism already.

The parking lot of the Slippery Lady was no better plowed out than it had been the week before. She didn't allow herself to hesitate before getting out of the van; her fear and revulsion of the place were real, and to get past them she had to keep moving.

She pushed open the claptrap door to the bar and had to blink hard to adjust to the smoky dimness. All conversation stopped when she closed the door behind her, and her hands abruptly turned to ice. It was even more crowded than usual. The bartender was a woodpecker of a man with a shiny face, a thin beak for a nose, and a helmet of soft black fluff for hair. A pair of toughs who had been arguing in a booth stopped to stare at her. A salesman was brooding over his liquid lunch; a trio of Chicanos raised speculative eyebrows at her; a tall black man in the corner didn't bother to turn around; and there was a giant at the far table in the shadows who was intimidating by his size alone even though she couldn't really see him. She tried to look at no one and everyone as she searched for Gramps, desperately praying that this time he wouldn't be there and she could walk right back out again. . . .

But he was there. She walked past the catcalling whistles and the steady male stares. Her teeth just bit at her bottom lip as she heard a chair scrape behind her. Gramps was slumped very peaceably on a table in the back. A whistling snore, the pale eyes closed, his whisper-soft hair so dear, that big emerald winking at her from his ring finger . . . She took a breath and bent down. "Gramps?" she whispered.

His soft blue eyes opened obediently. Abruptly, he slung an arm affectionately around her, throwing her off-balance. Her purse clattered awkwardly to the floor, and she heard a snicker behind her. Her teeth clenched together. She took an instant to smooth back a strand of her chin-length hair and then moved swiftly. The overcoat on the rack by the booths was Gramps. She reached the rack but could not make it back to her grandfather before one of the Chicanos laid a hand on her arm. She didn't need to speak Spanish to understand his basic message.

She shook her head and moved to pass him. He grabbed for her arm again, and she stood stone-still, her gray-blue eyes turning to ice. "I said *no*. Got it?"

The hand dropped, but the man still stood there. She whirled around, afraid he would see just how terrified she was. From the back of her head, she saw another big shadow getting up and swallowed. She hated all of it. Maybe none of them meant any harm, but it turned her stomach to be the best entertainment the bar had had all day. She took the coat back to Gramps.

The bartender was leaning over the counter, his mouth pursed in disgust and indignation. "Next time you just talk him into having his Friday afternoon bout on his own side of town, sweetheart," he warned her. "We've had enough of it. I run a respectable bar here—"

Loren stiffened, her face turning chalk-white. "He didn't break anything?" she inquired quietly, aware that everyone in the place was listening.

The bartender's voice rang out loud and clear. "That's not the point. Next time I might just be calling the police—"

Her vulnerable eyes turned haunted. "Please . . . I . . ."

"Lay *off* her!" The furious voice came from behind her . . . and a distance up. Six foot three of up. By some miracle, everyone else seemed to have suddenly settled back in their seats, minding their own business again, not looking. For an instant, she stared at the bartender, who looked as shocked as she did that anyone had taken up her cause in a place where people seemed to enjoy trouble. The woodpecker's mouth was open; he promptly closed it.

She glanced back at the giant and then did a double take. Not many people had the same rusty shade of hair that she did. His, though, had a peppering of silver at the temples. The man was huge and had a face that belonged in the bar . . . and yet didn't. She saw the two scars on his face and the frame that could take care of itself in any dark alley; she'd heard the gravelly voice, but there was still something wrong . . . his eyes. It was his eyes that didn't fit. The dark green gaze was sharp, intelligent, oddly compelling, and aimed straight at her. "I'll help you out with him," the rough voice offered.

Rapidly, she regained her poise. "Thank you, but I can take care of my own," she said crisply. Which had approximately as much effect as fending off an atomic attack with a BB gun. The pair of green eyes said as much. The stranger's size and stature said he could do as he damn well pleased, and at the moment he was holding her grandfather's coat. She snatched it, leveling a steady cold stare at Sexy Eyes before turning back to her grandfather. "Come on, darling," she coaxed.

William Shephard stirred, waking with a wide-open smile. "My darlin' Loren . . . and haven't I been telling you not to be comin' here? Sure, and . . ." The Irish monologue went on and on. She managed to get one of his arms through a coat sleeve and then, with one knee on the bench, she leaned in front of her grandfather to try to angle the rest of the coat behind him. It wasn't easy. One could have heard a pin drop in the place; the stranger was still standing behind her, and her hands were shaking.

"I would like another drink before we go."

"Yes, Gramps." She managed with strange ease to get the other arm in the remaining sleeve, only to realize he had divested himself of the first.

"There's someone behind you, darlin'."

"Yes, Gramps." She gave up, awkwardly got the coat completely off again, blew a wisp of auburn hair from her cheek, and buttoned up her grandfather's suit jacket instead. "Are we ready, sweetheart?"

"Are we ready . . . ?" Her grandfather focused dizzily on the giant behind her.

"Buck," the man supplied.

"Buck," Gramps echoed. "You help Loren. She shouldn't be here. I've told her over and over . . ."

"Yes, Gramps," Buck replied in an exact parody of her own patient voice.

Any other time, Loren might have smiled. But now, exhausted and exasperated, she flashed him a baleful look. Those dark green eyes were just waiting for her, far too bright for a man who had presumably been drinking all afternoon. The fabric of his black turtleneck, now frayed, was nevertheless of good quality. Excellent quality. Hard times? She worked with too many blue-collar laborers to be wary simply because of rough features and size, but there was something about the way he looked at her that caused a prickling at the back of her neck, like cat fur.

"Come on, darling." She put one of Gramps's arms over her shoulder and attempted to maneuver him out of the booth.

"He's still got a bill to be settled here," the bartender called out belligerently. The giant faced him with a level stare, and the bartender's voice promptly lowered two polite octaves. "Actually, miss, it's only for that last drink..."

She slapped two dollars down on the bar, but even in the few seconds that transaction had taken, the scene seemed to have gotten away from her. The stranger had Gramps easily pinned under one shoulder, and the two of them seemed to be headed for the door whether she came or not. Loren snatched up her purse and scurried ahead of the two men, opening the door, blowing away yet another wisp of auburn hair from her face. Her features were flushed, her eyes silvery gray. There was stubbornness in the lift of her chin. No matter how desperately she needed the giant's help, she felt wary. This character was a simple good Samaritan the way she was a linebacker for the Detroit Lions.

Behind her, in the two minutes it took to reach the van, Gramps was trying to tell his life story. Hurriedly, she unlocked the side of the van and swung both doors open. She waited, unconsciously lifting one foot after the other, in the slushy parking lot. It was wickedly freezing; a bitter gust of wind strained at her coat, slashing it open to reveal the powder-blue wool skirt hugging the curve of her thighs. The man who called himself Buck glanced briefly at her, then he was busy settling her grandfather in the back of the van. Gramps was still talking.

"Buck just said he'd come to dinner, Loren. Knows all about the horses, he does, the sulkies... A good man, don't think I can't tell. 'Xactly the kind of man you nee—"

"Yes, Gramps. " Oh, Lord! she thought.

"I like him, Loren. Got stranded here without a car, he did. We'll help him out. Buck, you take care of my Loren, now..."

Buck—or whatever his name was—finally came out of the van as Gramps was dropping off again. He turned to her, apparently waiting. Surely, he hadn't taken any of the conversation seriously. What was he waiting for?

"Thank you. I really appreciate your help." He was still waiting. She tried to laugh. "Of *course* you must have a car," she informed him.

Something flickered in his eyes, an expression of humor that quickly turned grim again. "Is your grandfather likely to be ill on you?" But he didn't wait for the answer. "Actually, I do seem to be stranded here for the moment. Why don't we just get your grandfather home? I'll take care of myself from there."

"Well . . ." She didn't believe him. That man had *never* been stranded, but still she found herself wavering. There were times when it was no joke getting her grandfather home and into the house. She sighed unhappily. A very bad decision was probably in the making, but he *was* there. "Perhaps if you would just ride home with us in case he . . . I would pay you," Loren said swiftly, "and I'll also give you the taxi fare back to . . . wherever it is you're going."

Another fleeting expression of amusement crossed his face. "I think I can manage . . . without your having to pay me anything."

"It would only be fair," she insisted. What exactly was he finding so funny? She changed her mind completely about asking him a second and a half later. The van wasn't particularly fancy, but there was a couch in back and carpet up to the two front seats. Ample room—at least until the huge stranger came up to sit next to her after closing the doors. He took up an incredible amount of space. His long legs barely had stretch room, and the crown of his rusty head almost touched the ceiling. She started the engine with misgivings. She must have been temporarily insane to accept this man's unexpected offer of help with Gramps. "Listen," she started firmly.

"He reminds me of someone. My Aunt Emma," the man mused as he turned down his coat collar and relaxed, his eyes staring straight ahead. "I used to dread her Saturday afternoon teas. Prim and proper as England she was, until tea time. By the time she was through putting medicine in her cup, she could swear like a soldier and snore like a dragon. Just on Saturdays, mind you."

Unwillingly, Loren found herself almost smiling. So this hulking stranger had a little empathy and a lot more perception than most people. Maybe she wasn't the only one who had this sort of problem.

"Now Aunt Emma was straight-laced Boston to the core. Only on Saturdays did she suddenly get a French accent," the man continued gravely.

Loren did smile then, relaxing. "Gramps's ancestry is English and French. We're only Irish on Friday afternoons."

She swung out of the driveway and faced a steady stream of Friday Livernois traffic. Detroit traffic had a distinctive personality, particularly on the expressway headed toward the northern suburbs. It was kill or be killed, with no one particularly interested in the outcome. Too preoccupied to concentrate on her driving, Loren heard a horn blare behind her as she rapidly switched lanes; but by the time she glanced in the rearview mirror, it was to check on Gramps rather than the irate driver. A semi-truck loomed ahead of her, and she swerved again, passing on the right this time, trusting that the rest of the cars behind her would understand. "I do appreciate your stopping to help," she told the man beside her. "Most people wouldn't have." She paused. "My sister will be home . . . and the housekeeper. As soon as we get to the house, I'll phone a taxi for you."

"If we get there in one piece."

"Pardon?" Her eyebrows lifted pertly in inquiry.

He motioned her eyes rapidly back to the road. "You can either pass that car ahead or hit him."

He needn't sound so critical. Crossly, she speeded up and passed the turtle-slow car. "Better?" she said stiffly.

"My mother used to tell me that we're all on earth on borrowed time, but I had a little longer rental in mind. How did you ever pass driver's training?"

"Gramps bribed the cop," she said smoothly.

It shut him up quite nicely, but she couldn't miss that slash of a smile. He really wasn't a brawler type at all when he smiled. In fact, with those beautiful eyes... He was staring at her so intently that she flushed and quickly riveted her gaze on the highway, deciding she had imagined that certain kind of interest in his eyes. It was impossible. She didn't need a mirror to know she undoubtedly looked as though she'd just come very close to unraveling—which she had. "As I said," Loren repeated, "we have a live-in housekeeper. She does have a bad back, though, and if you wouldn't mind helping me get Gramps into the house..."

"I heard you the first time. There'll be an audience, so I should stop thinking about robbery and rape. Immediately."

She lapsed back into brooding silence. Very funny. But the man was *not* what he seemed. Out of work, perhaps, but he spoke in educated accents and was too damned quick on the uptake for comfort. This associaton wasn't going to be a long one. She carried few scars from her short-term marriage seven years ago, but there was a lingering wariness when she couldn't place a man. And since placing men was her job, the enigmatic Buck was beginning to get under her skin. She put on her professional voice as she turned off the expressway. "It's a rough economy for everyone these days," she said with impersonal sympathy. "Have you been out of work long?"

Those bushy eyebrows lifted. "What makes you think I'm out of work?"

She shrugged, stopped for a red light, and reached down to turn off the heater. "In *that* bar in the middle of a Friday afternoon? Construction?" she guessed.

"I— At times." He hesitated, and she could feel his eyes on her, a little too shrewd for comfort. "I was in the bar to meet an old friend I went to school with. When we were teenagers, it was a different kind of place. Not better, just different. I hadn't been back there in so long..."

"Of course," she said smoothly. She believed part of his

story. She could visualize him as a black-leather-jacketed teenager with a fake ID, busy being tough. But the rest of what he was trying to convey, that he was not normally in a bar on a Friday afternoon . . . well.

"Somehow I had the feeling you weren't going to believe me," he murmured wryly.

"I never said that!"

"You didn't have to." He paused. "Could you try to believe I haven't been in a brawl since I was sixteen?"

"Really, I . . ."

"It's a big lag, between sixteen and thirty-six. I can't decide which is more ridiculous—the image of you in that bar looking like a virgin in a brothel or the image of me trying to remember how to land a left hook in the face of the meathead who was hassling you. Not that I find either image amusing," he said flatly.

She floundered in the quick little silence that followed, flashing back to the moment when he'd come up from behind her and the trouble had dissipated like docile little waves on a quiet sea. She could pinpoint it as the moment her hands had stopped shaking. He sounded angry that she had been in the bar in the first place; she didn't know what to make of that, but she groped rapidly to take charge of the conversation again. "I used to think that anyone who really wanted work could find it, but that certainly hasn't been true lately."

"I take it you're gainfully employed?"

"I'm a personnel manager. Though for how long . . . I'd like to say I could offer you a job, but with things as they are . . ." She felt an involuntary surge of compassion toward him. Whatever else he was, he didn't look like a man who enjoyed being on the unemployment line.

"It's perfectly all right." The gravelly voice had a sudden cryptic undertone. She glanced at him curiously, but then a horn beeped behind her. The light had turned green.

"I didn't mean to offend you," she said quietly.

"You didn't. But why do I keep getting the feeling that you feel safer thinking I'm on the welfare rolls?"

His half-smile seemed mocking, and she didn't care for his tone at all. "Don't be ridiculous," she said crisply. "First of all, I feel perfectly safe. Obviously. You just went out of your way to help me, at a time when most people would have looked the other way. So—"

"I'm glad," he said swiftly.

"Pardon?"

"That you feel so safe."

She refrained from gritting her teeth. All right, she didn't feel safe. She felt absolutely stupid driving home with a perfect stranger twice her size sitting beside her. But he didn't have to rub her nose in it.

"Tell me about your training in karate," he consoled her. "It might make you feel better."

For an instant, she bristled with an absolute fury, but it subsided just as quickly. Totally against her will, she found herself chuckling. "Four years," she said blandly. "A black belt, of course. I've won world tournaments. Not karate, judo—you know, the bigger the opponent, the harder he falls? It's a distinct disadvantage for the enemy to be larger; you use his weight against him, you see . . ."

When she was done describing her mythical judo skills, he was laughing. They both subsided into silence. "Feel better?" he asked after a time.

For no rational reason, she did, she realized, frowning. Was it because despite herself this man intrigued her, or because she was relieved that they were going to be on her doorstep within the next five minutes and she would be rid of him?

Chapter

2

LOREN WAS UNIQUELY conscious of Buck's appraisal as she turned into the winding driveway that led to the Shephard house. At first glance, the grounds implied wealth and grace, but a closer scrutiny revealed that the paved drive had pocked and not been fixed, that the old asphalt tennis court hadn't seen a tennis ball in a very long time and was now so overgrown it was no longer likely to. The house rose in two old-fashioned stories, an overhanging eave with pillars in front, the southern side shaded with maples and white oak in the summertime. The garage was separate, and though it was capable of holding four cars, her van wouldn't fit under any of the low ceilings. Not that she would bring this to Buck's attention, she thought as she drove the van up to the front door for the ease of getting Gramps out.

But surely as he looked at the house, Buck couldn't help noticing that the paint was peeling rather wretchedly in spots. She'd managed the doors and lower windows the summer before, but painting the rest of the house had eluded both her salary and ability. Yet despite its dilapidated air,

15

she loved the place more than she loved any human being, barring Gramps, and she could never let it go.

Buck's eyes had been scanning ever since they turned into the private driveway, and Loren felt a moment's unease. If he wasn't scrutinizing the peeling paint, he could very well be thinking there would be valuable heirlooms to steal in a house like this. The thought faded as he got out of the van. He just didn't seem like a thief. Danger came from that giant in other ways... In a moment, he had the side doors open and was angling out a newly talkative Bill Shephard.

Loren opened the front door and stepped in just ahead of them. "Angie?" she called. On inspiration, she added, "Joan?" Even a fictitious housekeeper had to have a name.

The hallway was square, leading to a massive dining room on the right and a living room on the left. The entire downstairs was carpeted in a soft moss green that had been plushly elegant at one time; with the careful placement of furniture Loren had hidden most of the threadbare spots. Duncan Phyffe tables in the living room were matched by traditional couches and chairs in cream and a light federal blue. It was a huge room, and perhaps to someone more affluent than her unexpected guest, the furnishings would look a bit sparse, making it obvious that pieces had been sold as the need occurred. She didn't personally mind the austerity, and anyway, beyond were the open French doors to the library, a room that radiated her favorite kind of clutter: books, paintings, and roomy furniture meant to curl up in.

"ANGIE?" She sighed when there was still no answer. She felt uncomfortable having to motion Buck upstairs with Gramps; had her sister been there, she would have felt less uneasy.

Buck seemed to wield the frail old body of her grandfather as if William Shephard weighed less than a sack of potatoes; the old man had fallen asleep again. Loren led the way up, feeling increasingly awkward. The stranger hadn't even seen the kitchen, and now he was on the way to the bedrooms.

"It's the last door on the left..." There were six bedrooms and three baths, massive, old-fashioned rooms that led off the ballroom of a hall. The doors were all oak and heavy with crystal knobs. High-vaulted ceilings and alcoved cubbyholes...For some ridiculous reason, she wanted the stranger to like the place and not notice the holes in the carpet or the barren spots on the walls where paintings had obviously been taken down.

Whatever his thoughts, they undoubtedly flew out of his mind at the sudden emergence of a tall blond bombshell clothed in a pale pink slip with a brush in her hand from one of the bedrooms. Loren glared at her sister, but Angela ignored her basilisk gaze as she said, "Honestly, Loren, I *am* sorry about this afternoon. I got home from classes at noon, and I was so tired—oh!" As the sweetest blue eyes heaven made were bestowed on the towering virile form of the giant, appreciation promptly replaced shock. Curiosity and perhaps amazement followed as Angela looked at Loren with raised eyebrows. *You?* her look seemed to say.

"In there." Loren motioned Buck irritably to her grandfather's bedroom. It was hardly a moment for introductions.

"I won't be here for dinner, Lor. I'm going out with David, so you won't have to cook for me. I knew you'd find Gramps. I really think this time you should consider—"

"NO!"

Loren followed Buck into the bedroom. When her grandfather was flat on the bed, she started taking off his shoes. Buck was working on the buttons of his suitcoat. And Angie, Loren noted, appalled, was casually in the doorway as if she were fully dressed. "It's been the most dreadful day. The hot water's out again—and I was just going to do the dishes. So I couldn't do that *or* take a shower... Do you need any help?" she asked virtuously.

By now Gramps was already beneath a blanket. Loren straightened up, brushed her hair away from her face, and honored her sister with a level stare. "Behave yourself," she said evenly. "His name is Buck, and he's already seen that you have an outstanding figure, so unless you want to freeze to death, you might as well put on some clothes."

Angela's eyes widened. "You're certainly not in a very good mood."

"No," Loren agreed, "I'm not."

"Well then, I'll just leave you two to have a cup of coffee or something." Her eyes lingered one more appreciative moment on Buck, then she asked with a frown, "Who's Joan? I thought I heard you calling—"

"Our housekeeper," Loren said flatly.

One could not accuse Angela of being slow. "Oh," she said brightly, reaching out to pat her sister's shoulder as if to comfort the demented. Then she sashayed barefoot from the room with a swivel of one pink satin hip.

Loren turned to find a silent Buck with a peculiarly contorted face. He was standing with his hands jammed comfortably in his pockets, his shock of rusty hair rumpled from the wind, his stark green eyes all over her like a camera. She had the peculiar impression that he was close to either laughter . . . or anger.

"I'm Miss Prim, and that's Miss Hot and Heavy. In case you haven't guessed. Anyway, welcome to the household, Buck," she said wearily. "Somehow, I even have the insane urge to offer you a cup of coffee. But please don't steal anything, okay? I'm too tired even to call the police if it came to it."

The kitchen was a huge square with a thousand cupboards and the most inefficient of all possible working settings, but the room was light, and the huge old oak table had character. Except for Angela's excess of dishes, the room was spotless. Impatiently, Loren went first to the sink and filled it with soapy water. She set the dishes in to soak, not to make a suitable impression on the man who had followed her to the kitchen, but simply because she couldn't stand dirty dishes.

Buck moved behind her, lifting the teapot to make sure

it contained water, then turning on the burner beneath it. "Coffee and cups?" he questioned quietly.

"You'll have to move the kettle to the back burner. That one doesn't work," she said irritably. "Cups are just above you, and instant coffee's on the side there."

"Come here to peace and quiet every night, do you?" he asked dryly as he obeyed her instructions.

"I manage."

"You're the sole support for all three of you?"

She flashed him a withering glance, then returned to the dishes in the sink. "I manage," she repeated. "Angela will be out of school in June." She rinsed the dishes, stacked them in the drainer, and wiped her hands hurriedly on a dishcloth, then bent over in front of the refrigerator to take out the casserole she'd made that morning. Belatedly, she remembered that her grandfather had promised Buck dinner, and she looked up at him guiltily. That whole thing was absurd, of course, but Buck seemed as conscious of the casserole she was holding as she was. "I'm sure you really don't want to stay for dinner," she told him, hoping she didn't sound rude. "I'll be happy to offer you coffee, and then I'll call a taxi—"

"I really would appreciate a meal," he contradicted her pleasantly.

Which was just it. He looked . . . hungry. The whistle on the tea kettle sputtered just as she stepped forward to put the casserole in the oven, and both she and Buck suddenly tried to fill the same space at the same time. She felt a rock-hard thigh against hers, then the most incredible sensation of a large, possessive hand on the curve of her hip, steadying her. Loren gave a small jump backward, feeling heat rush through her veins instead of blood. He was just so . . . virile-looking . . .

"Loren," he said gently, "take off your coat."

He pulled the kettle from the offending stove, the noise ceasing immediately. She looked down at herself with a flush and started unbuttoning, but then stopped as she remembered the casserole and put it in the oven.

So take off your coat, she told herself. What is *wrong* with you? But she knew what was wrong. It was the powder-blue sweater and skirt, which clung like sin to the slim curves of her hips and showed off a frankly sensational pair of legs. The outfit had rated her a dozen catcalls in the plant all day—which had made her laugh. This man made her feel differently . . . Why should the thought that he might find her diminutive figure to his liking disturb her so? Obviously, she was suffering a momentary bout of insanity.

She came back from putting away her coat without looking at him, poured the coffee into mugs, and transferred them to the table.

"Your hands are shaking. How often does that happen—the scene in the bar?"

Her chin lifted. "I manage." She didn't add that she'd had enough questions from a man whom she'd met in a derelict saloon, or that she was furious that he'd noticed her trembling hands. Well, that bar *was* shudder material; it inevitably caught up with her.

Buck sipped his coffee standing, glancing out at the yard and around the room. "You want me to look at your hot-water heater?"

"Pardon? Oh, no, of course not. I can man—"

It didn't seem wise to finish as she caught those eyes fixed on her like dark jade. She could have sworn she heard a low warning growl in his throat. "I know. You can *manage,*" he bit off. "In the meantime, you're going to sit down and put your feet up and do absolutely nothing for a few minutes while I go down to the basement and look at that heater. Aren't you?"

"I— Yes." Evidently. She sat absolutely still for several minutes, staring at the open basement door through which he'd disappeared. One would almost think he was genuinely concerned about her, when of course there was no reason to be. Or perhaps he just had a fetish about hot-water heaters?

"I closed the door to Joan's room," he said blandly when he came back up. "Told her to take the evening off. The hot-water heater needs a new coil; it'll have to wait until morning." He held up a sort of coiled rectangle, corroded with white limey deposits.

She resisted the urge to tell him that if he were 5'1" and ninety-nine pounds, he, too, might have invented some protection. Instead, she said pleasantly, "Good. Joan's overworked."

"I'll just bet she is," he agreed. "This is too big a house for one person to take care of."

And if he weren't so big, she'd hit him. She was about to say that she managed very well, but decided against it. He smiled approvingly, as if he'd read her mind.

Angela strolled in as Loren was serving dinner for herself and Buck. In a brilliant red peasant blouse and skin-tight black pants, she looked ready to seduce from a streetcorner. Her blond hair cascaded to her shoulders in waves as she pirouetted prettily. "Like the blouse?" she asked, seemingly to both of them at once.

Loren studied her sister. Angela wasn't beautiful, but without question she exuded a special brand of sensuality. A dangerous brand. Loren worried about her sister on an every-five-minute basis, but her tactfully phrased admonitions only seemed to fuel Angela's rebellion. At any rate, this evening was hardly the time for another lecture. "It's new, isn't it? Where are you going, honey?" she asked.

"Just to a movie. What do you think?" she asked Buck.

"That depends on whether you like your David or are just going out with him to attract other men," Buck answered smoothly.

"Pardon?" Used to immediate and unqualified approval from all males, Angela suddenly looked the very young woman she was.

"It's a lovely blouse," Buck assured her, "but when I care about the woman I'm with, I'd rather she didn't attract other male attention—at least deliberately. I'd rather have her to myself. But then maybe this David is nothing important to you."

Angela suddenly looked stricken, a measure of how important David actually was to her, and she glanced down at the blouse and pants again. "Why, I wouldn't . . . You don't think he'd suspect I was trying to come on to someone else, do you?" she asked Buck seriously.

"I don't believe you're having this conversation with a total stranger," Loren said helplessly.

"But that's just the point," Angela said defensively, turning again to Buck. "So you really think . . ."

Two changes of clothes later, Loren was astonished to see her sister leave in a plain navy-blue sweater that dated two years back and actually had a measure of breathing space in it. David Brown was let in, greeted, and the pair left as Loren and Buck were finishing dinner.

"I hope the young man has honorable intentions," Buck said dryly as the car lights splashed across the kitchen window and then disappeared. It was, to Loren's surprise, already dark.

"By some miracle," Loren said wryly, "David's a winner. His dad owns a hardware store, and David's taking a year of business courses at a local college before joining him. Not to say that I'm naive enough to think David's devotion to my sister is based on an appreciation of her mental abilities. Angela's most eloquent communications tend to be, shall we say, nonverbal?"

Buck nodded, leaning back comfortably with one of his feet cocked on the rung of a chair, sipping coffee. "And you? Are you equally eloquent with your . . . anatomy?"

"No, of course n—" The answer came out so easily that she blinked. "Now you just listen here!"

"You're certainly safe as church this evening then," he interrupted her blandly. There was a sea of humor in his narrowed green eyes as she sputtered for the appropriate put-down. "You're old enough," he said dryly, "and you've got the looks. Or is that what terminated that short-term marriage of yours?"

"How on earth did you even know I was—"

"Gramps," he said helpfully. "On that long ramble between the bar booth and the back of the van."

"For your information, Mr. Busybody, seven years ago

I separated from my husband of six months because he didn't like to work and I did, and the only thing that held us together that long was our sex life. Is there anything else you wanted to know?" Loren snapped furiously.

"Actually . . ."

"Actually, I think it's past time you were headed home."

"*Actually*, I think it's time you checked on your grandfather."

When exactly had that craggy half-smile altered to something else? Suddenly, there was naked appraisal in his eyes when she stood up, as if he were just now letting her know that he had noticed every detail of the powder-blue outfit. And suddenly he had grooves on his forehead she hadn't noticed before, an iron chin of assurance . . . Telling this man he had a lot of nerve would be like bouncing a marshmallow off a steel wall. She felt an unfamiliar instinct of danger, suddenly aware not only that he had managed to find out almost everything about her in a very short time, but that she was not entirely immune to his humor, to his lazy way of taking charge, to the . . . look of him. "Listen," she said firmly, "I *am* going to check on my grandfather, but when I come back—"

"I'll call the taxi as soon as you return," he assured her, and she stared at him momentarily before stalking out of the room and heading upstairs.

Her fingers massaged an ache at the back of her neck as she walked. This Black Friday was beginning to take its toll on her. She leaned against the doorway to her grandfather's room, the hall light casting a soft halo on his sleeping shadow. Exhaustion hit her at once, like the bullet of a sniper.

William Shephard was sleeping the sleep of the innocent. His wife had no longer died on a Friday fourteen years ago. His son and daughter-in-law hadn't been killed in a yachting accident. The family business sustained for nearly a century had not disintegrated in his hands. He was curled up like a child, and as Loren looked at him, she felt a pit of pain inside trying to burst. Gramps was seventy-four, and she loved him, and she was totally powerless to help him.

Her eyes closed, and the days ahead stretched out in wretched weariness in her mind. Two weeks of double work were coming up at the plant, and every day of the fortnight was filled to the brim with other people's troubles. The scene at that horrid bar still grated on her nerves; how she hated the sleaziness of the place, all the men's eyes on her . . . Her failures suddenly pressed in on her—her marriage, for one, Gramps, for another, and surely somehow she should have managed to control Angela, force to her sister to accept some badly needed discipline . . . Then there was the house. Everything seemed to be going at once, and there was just no way her salary could be stretched far enough to meet every need . . .

She could manage, she'd told Buck. Well, she had and she could; nothing was going to get her down. Nevertheless . . .

She walked slowly back down the stairs and pushed open the revolving door to the kitchen. Buck was leaning back against the counter, his hands shoved lazily in his pockets. He projected an easy, careless strength, a ton more than any one person needed, and not only brute power, but also a mental steel that just seemed to come with the man. She suddenly coveted that strength desperately and could feel something inside of her start to slip that she just never let slip . . .

"I want you to go now." She intended to sound very firm, to use the dismissive tone for which she was famous at work. Instead, even to her own ears, her voice sounded hoarse and even pleading.

He was across the room in two seconds. "The hell you do," he growled.

Chapter
3

LOREN COULDN'T IMAGINE how it happened. She *never* cried, and once the tears started, she was horrified when they wouldn't stop. Her throat clogged up, and her eyes simply kept flooding . . . she was just so exhausted; it had been such a wretched, wretched day. Suddenly, Buck was there, encouraging her face to his chest, offering a comfort like riches in his silence and the gentle strength of his arms. He scooped her into his arms, found his way by some streak of fate to her favorite rocker in the library, and cradled her to his lap in that dark room, and rocked. One long arm circled her close, his fingers resting on the slim curl of her hip; the other hand very slowly smoothed back her hair, over and over.

"I feel so ridiculous," she burbled miserably.

"There's nothing ridiculous about crying," he said gently. "You're unhappy, Loren. Good Lord, I don't know how you handle all of it—"

"I am *not* unhappy!" she thundered between sobs.

"All right. You are *not* unhappy," he echoed patiently.

With some effort, he dredged up a handkerchief from his back pocket, first mopping her face and then holding it over her nose. "Blow," he ordered.

She was mortified. "I do *not* have to blow my nose!"

"Of course you do."

"You've been driving me crazy from the minute I set eyes on you!" she accused him and, snatching the handkerchief away from him, blew her nose. "You think I regularly invite strangers home? It's all your fault. You . . . confused me. And I *never* cry. *Certainly* never on some—"

"Stranger's lap?" he supplied readily.

"You may find all of this very funny—"

"Loren, it's obviously not a rational day for you. You might as well give in to your feelings . . ."

She tensed like a coil when his head came down. Their lips met at an awkward angle, a whispery tease of softness in the dark. His fingers twined in her hair, encouraging her neck back, and the next kiss was less sweet, with a coaxing hunger as his mouth covered hers, his hand on the smooth arch of her throat. She was very still, an instinct of danger rushing through her bloodstream, an awareness of how potent the blend of darkness, the man, the moment, and the weakness inside her. His lips lifted, brushed hers again more lightly. "You're no virgin, Loren," he said hoarsely. "Give me your mouth. You know what I want, give it to me."

Though gently spoken, the order startled her. In her world, she was the one who gave gently spoken orders. While she was figuring out what it felt like to have her own game turned against her, his mouth fastened on hers, arching her neck back, his tongue searing inside her parted lips. The dizziness was so unexpected that she reached up to grasp his head, his hair vibrantly alive in her splayed hands, the texture so rich it curled around her fingers. One of his hands roamed from her thigh to the soft roundness of her hip, molding her closer to him.

She didn't shy away until he moved up, caressing her

ribcage. One of her slim hands tried to cover his then, tried to push him away. She was sensitive about her small breasts and always had been. And there was another reason she shied instinctively...

His hand didn't seem to understand denial. It soothed and gentled and coaxed and teased all the surrounding flesh, and finally closed in on what it wanted at the same time that a helpless little murmur escaped from her throat. Her breast, so tender and vulnerable, seemed to swell in an effort to fit his huge hand. Like lightning, she felt suddenly let loose, the pressure of her mouth matching his as her fingers tightened in his hair, a tension she knew he could feel in her thighs.

He knew. He was not the kind of man to worry about silver when he'd found gold. He coveted that response, kneading her soft breast until she was trembling, until her back arched for the touch of him and there seemed nothing but sweet wildness in her veins. He was too smart, her stranger. If he'd go back to caressing her thigh, she could go back to feeling like warm melted butter. As it was, she felt on fire, and he was deliberately fanning those flames, obviously taking pleasure from her pleasure....

There was moisture on his forehead when he stood up and slowly lowered her to her feet. When she was steady, he severed all contact abruptly, breathing heavily as he left the room.

Loren stood still in the darkness. She felt like hot honey inside, and the sensation left her bemused and a little ashamed. Buck was back in a moment, holding two coats, and they put them on in silence.

It was freezing outside, black-cat dark, moonless. Tree limbs stretched stark and naked to the sky, the ground was still layered with snow except for the drive itself. She expected... she didn't know what. Some comment from him, something awkward.

It just wasn't that way. They walked in the silence, pulse rates forced to normal, breathing deeply of the frigid air. Even before she was cold, he had enfolded her just beneath his shoulder, snuggling her warm and close, but there was no longer any danger in his closeness.

"You're so damned small," he complained.

She smiled up at him. It was all going to feel very wrong at some point, but it didn't just yet. His arms felt like a gift.

"It won't always be this way, you know," he said finally. "Your grandfather, apart from his obvious problem, he isn't well, is he?"

"No," she admitted.

"And your sister will grow up. I look at her and thank God I'm not eighteen anymore. We offer up our weaknesses on a platter at that age; life's way of insuring we learn from experience, perhaps. You can't test the waters for her, Loren, not the waters she needs to test." He kissed her softly on the forehead and then stopped, burrowing her coat collar up around her neck before his arm circled her again.

"I hate money," she murmured absently.

"Pardon?"

"You're out of work, Buck, you can surely understand how hard it is to not have enough money. But we used to have too much of it in this family. Gramps stopped trying when he lost it. And Angela—only new clothes and stereos make her feel secure. My parents were killed on a boat that cost more than I make in ten years. Money . . . it sours people, confuses them . . . you can't know," she said bitterly. "My husband, too, was destroyed by it. Hal had more money than he knew what to do with. I tried to make our marriage work, but there just wasn't anything there. It was always solve every problem with money . . ." She hesitated. "You're different, Buck. I'm not trying to make something out of what happened in the library, so don't . . . worry. I'm not a clinger; I know you're about to walk out of my life, and that's fine. But I'd like to tell you . . ."

"Loren—"

The gravelly voice sounded disturbed, but she thought she understood. "No. I don't want to embarrass you. But you're real, Buck. You're not corrupted by that moneyed

world . . . Sometimes I feel like a character in a Tennessee
Williams play, trying to keep up this house when I know I
can't, caring for Gramps and Angela—"

"Stop it, Loren."

She stood on tiptoe and kissed his mouth softly, barely
noticing the sudden rigidity in his shoulders. "You haven't
got money, and I love you for that. I don't want a love
affair, and I haven't the time or energy for it if I did. Just
thank you, Buck. I needed your particular brand of man this
evening, and you came through better than anyone I've
known in a very long time."

They had reached the end of the driveway now, and she
extricated herself from his hold.

"You're dismissing me," Buck said, his tone almost
amused.

She nodded, smiling softly. "Good night, Buck."

The next morning Loren pulled on an old pair of jeans
and an equally old dark sweatshirt and tied a bandeau around
her hair. The thrilling agenda for this Saturday included
washing windows and scrubbing the kitchen floor. All morning as she rubbed at the window panes with cleaning fluid,
she kept seeing her reflection, the wildly curling hair around
the bandeau, the raggedy shirt, her face a smooth cameo
without makeup, all fresh-eyed and smiling. She looked ten
years old. She didn't care. The smiles just kept coming,
over absolutely nothing.

She didn't expect to see her giant stranger again. She
didn't want to see him. But that bizarre one-time encounter
had left her feeling strangely lighthearted, as though her
responsibilities had suddenly diminished, and her problems
had become a little less monumental than they'd been the
day before.

By one o'clock, she had a rag in her hand and a bucket
of soapy water on the kitchen floor. Her jeans were damp
at the knees when she stopped working for a minute and
inadvertently glanced out the kitchen window. Frowning,
she saw a gray pickup pull into the yard with LEEDS printed

on the side. Buck stepped out of the truck, wearing coveralls and carrying a package in his hands, and stalked toward the house with all the determination of the dominant male bulldozer that he was.

All Loren's lazy smiles of the morning abruptly died. As he reached the door, a kaleidoscope of emotions rushed through her, none of which she quite knew what to do with. "Buck, what on earth are you doing here? I hope you didn't steal the truck?" Loren accosted him as she half-opened the door. His eyes turned that dark jade she'd seen when he was angry in the bar yesterday; he was staring at the bucket on the floor and then at her ragged blouse and damp knees.

"Obviously, I must have borrowed it for the day."

She half-frowned, lips compressed, not opening the door any farther. He gave a sigh that sounded like a pent-up north wind, waiting for her to let him in.

"Look," she started carefully, "you must have misunderstood. I really don't think . . ."

A long metal rectangle urged its way through the slit in the door and clattered onto the counter. Next, a package of metal parts joined it.

"What is all this?"

"Payment for the free dinner yesterday," Buck said easily. "The coil for your hot-water heater. A gasket for the faucet to stop dripping. And a fuse for the burner on the stove. Now will you let me in so I can install them?"

Loren flushed. "That's very nice, but no thank you," she said firmly. "For one thing, it would be an imposition on your time. For another, you surely figured out that I can't afford to pay you. I appreciate the thought, Buck, but I really think it would be better all the way around if—"

She had to back up when he pushed the door open. When it closed behind him, there was the distinct reverberation of a near-slam. "Did anyone ever spank you when you were younger?" He handed her his coat, and she took it because it would have dropped on her wet floor if she hadn't.

"Now just listen here—"

"I'm unemployed, remember? There are no jobs to be

scouted out on a Saturday. So I've got nothing better to do, I wouldn't expect payment even if you offered it, and you're not going to stand there and deny you need a man around here."

She glared at him furiously. She knew what he had come back for, and it wasn't plumbing. She didn't blame him for misunderstanding, and she wasn't denying that she'd responded to him like some wanton little . . . whatever. Which was just the point. She needed no further complications in her life—she could barely handle what she had. "Just go away, Buck," she said in a low voice.

With a wicked glint in his eye, he said, "I don't think so."

She shrugged off the bandeau, letting loose a bounce of disheveled rusty curls. "You don't understand. The big thrill in my life is a bath on Sunday night. The rest of the days are filled from six in the morning until nine at night, and at nine I'm something between a zombie and a dead dishrag. Do you want to hear the schedule for today? Because I have a zillion things to do, and there's no one else to do them."

"I think you're presuming a hell of a lot, but I'm certainly willing to discuss your bath habits—any time," he assured her mildly, taking up the tool kit and parts packages. "It could just be that all I had in mind was fixing your hot-water heater." He was on his way downstairs before she had the chance to say another word.

Sure, stranger, her mind replied dryly. She stood still for a few moments, staring at the cellar door. and then stubbornly got down on her knees to finish the floor. A half-hour later she was done, but Buck was still in the basement. Angela had been in and out, discovered Buck's presence, and had gone down to keep him company. Gramps had been in and out, discovered Buck 's presence, and had gone down to keep him company. The Shephards were a very gregarious family, Loren thought wryly.

Determinedly, she filled a wicker basket with cleaning supplies. When the ground-floor rooms were dusted, she headed upstairs, and when she'd cleaned all the bathrooms there, she headed toward her own room. She had on a fresh pair of jeans and was pulling a soft wool sweater over her head when she heard the rap on the door. A full second later, he opened it.

"I seem to be looking for a badly behaving hairdryer."

Her coppery hair was wispy around her face from the static electricity of the sweater, and Loren knew he guessed she'd just pulled it on and was remembering exactly what was beneath it. He looked incongruous, that giant of a man in her mauve and white bedroom with its muted Monet prints. "Well, it's not in here," she said irritably.

Barefoot, she led the way to Angela's room, a screaming shout of color and youth—posters of punk-rock stars, an unmade bed, clothes strewn all over furniture and floor. She sighed. "Finding anything in here . . . Look, Buck you really don't have to do this . . ."

"It certainly would be a pity if your sister had to lift a finger herself around here," Buck said idly. "She gets off school at noon every day, you said?"

She flashed him a warning glance as she burrowed in the overcrowded closet for Angela's broken hairdryer. "She's had it rough, losing both our parents."

"You didn't lose the same two parents? She's spoiled," he said flatly.

"Fine," Loren snapped. "Handle her then, Buck—you certainly did a good job yesterday. Take over the whole damn house if you want, but I have to go out and get the groceries for the week. I'll say my good-byes now."

"Oh, I don't know. I'm getting a hell of a list from your two relatives. I may still be here when you get back."

She shoved the bulky hairdryer at him with a silver-eyed stare. "If you want to waste your Saturday, that's up to you. But don't count on conversation from me unless it's over the roar of a vacuum. I don't have time to play."

Chapter

4

BUCK EMERGED FROM the house just as Loren was coming up the driveway. She'd barely shut off the engine before he had the side doors of the van open. He managed three grocery bags to her one, toting them ahead of her wordlessly, and Loren found herself half-shaking her head. Dammit, what was she going to do about him? Why on earth was he doing all this?

The kitchen table was strewn with a pile of clean clothes, half-folded. She set down the grocery bag and her purse, taking off her coat even as she was starting to unpack the canned goods. A cup of coffee was whisked in front of her; she ignored it, working silently as Buck sat down at the table.

"You'll have hot water within the hour. The faucets upstairs and down are no longer dripping, and the burner on the stove's fixed. But the hairdryer is beyond repair, and your washing machine is going, Loren. There's a leak in the attic that could at least be token-patched from the inside, and the only thing wrong with your sister's stereo was a bent needle. Very mechanical, your family. I made out a list once I started the wash. It came to two pages. Actually, very few of these things are expensive if you don't have to pay a repair man for his time. And in the meantime," Buck continued mildly, "I threw out the slip with the hole in it. I knew damn well it was yours, your sister's things have 'brand new' all but written on them. The bras were easy to divide, but the panties I gave up on. They all stretch. You and your sister will have to sort out the rainbow. Perhaps Angela might even be able to rouse herself off that sweet little ass of hers..."

Loren smash-shut the vegetable bin, smash-shut the refrigerator, and turned to his expectant green eyes with her hands on her hips. "You are driving me NUTS."

Buck nodded mildly, as if the subject were of little interest to him. "I can't find your pajamas," he complained.

"I don't wear any."

"Cheaper that way?"

She drew in her breath, trying to contain the laughter that was bubbling up inside her. He had set up such a darned good show to prove his unusual (for a man) domestic skills— taking on her wash, indeed! Yet she couldn't laugh. Her pride was smarting from his help, she was no one's charity case and she didn't like anyone running interference for her. But... he *had* put in a three-day work week in a few hours, and professional help would have cost her a bundle she didn't have; she even felt a grudging respect for this man who pitched in with an energy and determination that matched her own, obstacles or no. She just couldn't seem to pigeonhole him—he seemed neither a nomadic Jack-of-all-trades nor the goodwill neighborly type.

"Who *are* you, Buck? What are you doing here?" she asked finally.

"Sit down and I'll tell you, after you answer the question about the pajamas."

"Pajamas? Oh..." She brought the coffee cup with her and sat down at the head of the table. It was her first chance to sit all day, and she could not help the weary sigh that escaped from her. "I sleep without pajamas because I have a deliciously secret fantasy sex life," she said ironically. "That's what you wanted to hear, isn't it?"

"Good girl," he said approvingly. With his elbows on the table, he leaned forward and gave a wry little shake of his head. "You really don't 'throw' off-balance easily, do you?"

"I work with more than four-hundred men," she responded smoothly. "You can't expect to take me unaware too easily. Now it's your turn."

"All right," he returned promptly. "I'm the president of a local die-cast company."

She blinked. She'd just said she couldn't be taken unaware, and he had managed it just that quickly. For an instant, she could see him as the executive he claimed to be, with those shrewd green eyes and take-charge arrogance, the way he walked and the way he held those shoulders of his. And then she chuckled.

"You don't believe me." He was clearly amused.

She shook her head, still chuckling, and picked up the now-cooled coffee to take a sip. "No, I don't, thank heaven," she said gently. "You've got the arrogance to run something, Lord knows, and anyone could tell you've got a decent education behind you. But that 'president' image reminds me of my husband . . . the snob appeal of a prestigious title, the social elite game, the little hobbies that only money can pay for. All the really honest emotions that can take place between two people become buried under the gold." His expression froze, and she raised her eyebrows at him, sorry she had mentioned her ex-husband. "I associate very selfish qualities with money; I already told you that," she said clearly. "And you haven't got them. Besides, I already know your story."

"Oh, you do?"

The longer he stared at her, the more she felt an unwilling sexual awareness of him creep up on her as it had the night before. The virile breadth of his shoulders and the strength of his features, a certain quiet way he moved, the lingering promise in the embrace that still haunted her. "You weren't laid off, and you didn't quit," she said quietly. "You were fired, Buck. It was a good job, the problem is that you need to work for yourself. You couldn't cut it under someone else's gun. It wasn't that you couldn't do the work—you were probably excellent at it—but you wouldn't snap when someone belted out an order. Right?"

Buck looked startled and then scraped back the kitchen chair as he stood up to get himself a cup of coffee. "I will tell you this. The only job I was ever fired from was for just that reason. And you're right, I don't take orders well from anyone but myself. Loren?"

She cocked her head at him questioningly.

"I like the game. For now. Maybe you do, too. It's like seeing myself through your eyes, without any past intruding, without any judgments made because of status or titles or appearances. But it shouldn't go too far. When you want an honest answer to any question..."

She stood up, too, carted her empty cup to the counter, and then finished putting away the last of the groceries. "I hear you," she said finally. "Maybe I just like the game, too, for now. I'd like to believe that I really don't care who you are or what you've done. That I can judge all I need to judge from the man I see, as far as trust or character or... anything that matters." He didn't answer, just came close to her when he set down his coffee cup. She could feel the sudden electricity crackle, the special awareness of a man's nearness that she so rarely felt. "Thank you for doing all that work today," she said swiftly. "I'd offer you a drink instead of coffee, but unfortunately we don't stock any liquor, as you might have guessed."

"I don't want any liquor," he growled.

"No. We both know what you want, heaven knows why," she said wryly, but there was a sadness in her silvery eyes. She turned away, bunching up the last of the grocery bags with a nerve-crunching noise that didn't last very long. She started to loop the folded clothes over one arm, piling them up to her chin, and with an exasperated sound from the back of his throat, Buck piled a load in his own arms and followed her up the stairs.

"You can't have it, Buck," she said without looking back at him. "I mean it. I had a broken heart once; it was the only thing I couldn't handle. I just don't play anymore. I haven't the time; I haven't the emotional energy. I've got too many people to take care of now, so don't ask me. Do me a favor and just go, would you? You can do better in a thousand ways, and I think you know it."

"Loren—"

He hurried to open the door ahead of her, and there was Angela just on the other side, startled in her own rush to get down the stairs. Her eyes widened on both of them, and then she grinned pertly. "Hey, hey," she scolded. "No men above the stairs but Gramps. Those are Loren's rules, you know."

Unaccountably, Loren flushed. Angela was not only quick but invariably had a one-track mind. "Where are you off to?"

"David's, naturally. Gramps is napping, so don't make too much noise, you two. I mean, two black sheep in the family are enough. Loren's our resident angel, Buck. You tarnish the title, and we won't like it."

"I can't imagine what you *think* you're talking about," Loren said tartly.

Angela only waved and sprinted past them down the stairs.

"Now all I need is for Joan to come up from the basement and start in," Buck complained as he trailed after Loren, who sorted through the piles of laundry and distributed the clothes room to room. "Your grandfather had at me while you were gone."

"Don't worry about it," she said shortly. "I can say my own no's very well, thank you."

"Had a lot of practice?"

"My fair share."

"From the four-hundred men you work with?"

"Among others."

"Anyone current?"

She walked into her bedroom and then turned around, pushing her hand firmly to his chest to shove him back out, closing the door. She heard his low-throated chuckling. All she wanted to do was run a quick brush through her hair and put on a fresh bit of lipstick . . . and gain two seconds of freedom. The stalk through the bedrooms had been fraught with undercurrents, verbal and physical. After a moment, she opened the door.

"I like your hair mussed, and I don't like you to wear lipstick," he said promptly.

"Those are your problems, not mine." But she was pleased.

"Anyone current?" he repeated.

"No," she said with exasperation. "How about you?"

He hesitated. "No one that matters."

"A sleeping partner," she guessed, and saw his jaw tighten. "I'll bet you have a lot of those."

"It took practice to become an outstanding lover."

She managed to look disappointed. "What a shame. I'm just not in that league; it's been too long. This day and age, though, I'm sure you can find someone in your own ballpark."

"Loren . . ."

She hurried ahead of him down the stairs. He followed her through the hall, through the kitchen's swinging door, through the kitchen itself, all the way to the back door, which she opened and then stood there. "No," she said firmly. "Now go home."

He took his time getting his coat from the kitchen chair and putting it on, his eyes never leaving hers. She met his look until he started walking toward her, and then almost helplessly she averted her eyes, her long black lashes spiking her cheeks as she waited for him to pass. When he was next to her, he crooked one finger beneath her chin to tilt it up. "I've heard that no," he said quietly. "You say it another way, Loren, and I'll believe you." Ever so gently his face bent toward hers, and like quicksilver, their lips met. An unwilling softness shone from her eyes by the time he took his mouth from hers. It was not a blush of innocence that colored her cheeks but the warmth from his closeness. "Say no now, Loren," he murmured roughly.

She shook her head and took a step back from him with her chin high. "I'm saying no, Buck, because it won't work. It *can't* work, with my life. I'm asking you to understand," she said pleadingly. "I'm asking you to honor that I mean it."

He stared at her for a long minute and then moved on and out, leaving her to close the door behind him.

Loren dialed the phone with the eraser end of her pencil, nodding a thank you as Janey entered with the day's letters to be signed. She angled the phone between ear and shoulder as she signed her name on the pages, too certain of her secretary's typing skills to check her work. The phone rang at the other end . . . and rang, and rang.

It was more than three minutes before she could force herself to hang up. Another Friday afternoon and Angela had absolutely sworn she would stay home; Loren had even bribed her sister with the use of the van for the evening . . . Janey buzzed her, and Loren pressed her intercom button.

"There's a first-aid call from the boiler room, and Ralph's not answering," the secretary explained.

"If there was a drop of blood involved, Ralph's probably fainted," Loren said dryly. "Okay, Janey, on my way."

Snatching up her tortoise-shell safety glasses, Loren bolted through three sets of revolving doors. Past the foremen's offices, past the divisional managers and production, and suddenly there were two dozen monster presses, the steady woosh and hiss as they opened and closed blending with the acrid smell of hot plastic. A variety of greetings were shouted at Loren as she passed. She was distinctly the only one in a feminine cream blouse with ruffles at the throat, a camel skirt, and three-and-a-half-inch heels that were illegal plant attire in every way. Most of the time she found it both ironic and amusing to be the plant's sole sex symbol, but for now she ignored the affectionate catcalls.

The boiler room was spotless, but the noise level just barely met standard. Loren resisted the urge to cover her ears as she crouched down by the reclining man and motioned away the four or five onlookers. "It's just a nosebleed, boys. Johnny has them all the time . . ."

With help, she got Johnny to the first-aid room, and a half-hour later she was dabbing a cold, wet cloth at the red spot on her shoulder as she walked toward the offices. Two doors later, she whirled around a corner to collide with a short, stocky, whiskered man, who laughed as he grabbed at her shoulders.

"Matt!"

"I've been trying to find you, sexy. I feel bad about leaving you with a double work load . . ."

"I thought you'd already left on vacation—"

"I'm leaving, I'm leaving. But I told Frank he was taking advantage, Loren. He loads work on you as though you're some kind of bottomless pit . . ."

Loren laughed and perched her glasses on top of her head. "Don't be silly. I can manage. Now don't you be worried; just give us a kiss and get out of here while you still can."

The kiss was a swift smack of affection, but from around the side of Matt's shoulder, she suddenly saw one hell of a broad-shouldered redhead and his sidekick, a smallish white-haired man whose eyes were pale blue—and sober, very sober. The two men were glaring at her.

"Have a super time, Matt. I have to go—"

"Be good, honey."

Matt was gone, and relief filled Loren's heart because Gramps was *here*, sober and safe, and there would be no trauma at that horrid bar this Friday. She threw her arms around him, her joy and relief so explosive there were almost tears in her eyes. "I'm *so* glad to see you! But what are you doing here, darling?"

"Yes. Well, what kind of a place *is* this you're working in? You kiss strange men in the middle of the hallways, and I heard what he called you . . ."

Loren's arm dropped. "What did who call me?" she asked, bewildered.

"I won't repeat it in mixed company," Bill Shephard said irritably. "Buck is mixed company, Loren. Now say hello and show us to your office. I want to talk to you."

The reason why Bill Shephard was sober this Friday had ice-cold, very dark green eyes. Loren hadn't expected to see him again. She'd given him a clear-cut no, and she'd given it twice. "Buck," she acknowledged softly.

Fleetingly, she wished that he *had* listened to her because suddenly all those sensible, practical reasons why she couldn't pursue a relationship seemed to elude her. Glad to see him? She felt ill, an attack of spring fever when it was still winter, a feeling of euphoric intoxication for no reason at all.

Truthfully, the look of him didn't justify those feelings. He wore a forest-green sweater that matched his eyes, gray flannel slacks, and a long grayish jacket, unbuttoned. His rusty hair was disheveled from the wind outside, and the steel in his sideburns was reflected in his expression. Don't push me, the set of his jaw told her, and she hadn't done anything at all.

"Your office," he reminded her.

Chapter
5

LOREN COULD SENSE Buck appraising her office the moment she closed the door. The gold carpet, and chairs set up for interviews were office standard. So was the gray metal desk— except that hers was painted yellow; splashes of yellow and orange hung from the picture behind it; and her philodendron was gradually stealing up the window. She saw just a slip of the ice in him thaw as he glanced around, and then his eyes settled on her. She thought wryly that he saw too much. Her tan skirt was . . . office standard. The pale ivory blouse was ruffled—her own brand of femininity, as in to hell with office protocol. Safety glasses functioned as a hairband rather than eye protection, and her heels were predictably high. Frank had fought a losing battle the first two years she'd worked here, trying to fit her to the mold.

"You go around kissing a whole lot of these employees of yours?" Bill Shephard said belligerently.

"Gramps, don't be silly. Matt's married. He has three children and another on the way. I've been working for him for more than four years—"

"And what about what he called you?"

"Honey?" Loren guessed, knowing Matt.

"You tell her, Buck."

"Sexy," Buck supplied readily.

Her soft charcoal eyes lifted uncertainly to his. His gaze still radiated the hardness of jade . . . yet he'd come back. Unconsciously she sensed he was half-angry at just being here, that he'd never in his life even considered pursuing a woman who'd told him no.

"I should have been paying more attention when you first took this job—"

Loren wrenched here eyes from Buck's back to her grandfather. "Gramps, the people who work here are all very nice—"

"By *people* I assume you mean *men*. I haven't seen a woman since we passed the receptionist at the front door. *Are* there any other women working here?" Gramps demanded.

"I keep most of them hidden in the back room." Loren said dryly.

"Loren, I'm in no mood for your brand of humor—"

"Well, you're touching on a sore point. Women. I mean, how ironic it would be for me, in my job, to be sexist. It took six months for the foremen to even consider putting a woman on a press, only to discover that women weren't exactly lining up to lift fifty pounds on piece rate and risk their fingernails in the presses—"

"We weren't in the *plant*. We were in the *offices*—"

"So you passed by Engineering. Most of that department was staffed long before Lee lost the war. The Civil War. Back when women couldn't vote, and all those poor whales got killed to make corsets . . ."

"LOREN."

She would have liked to tell him how rough it had been four years ago to be hired as the token female manager just to fill some legal criteria about affirmative action. Unfortunately, Gramps seemed definitely hung up on kisses in hallways. She glanced at Buck again. The ice was half-thawed; the corners of his mouth were even fighting a smile. She thought fleetingly that he could easily have gotten her out of this nonsensical war between the generations, that surely *he* had not mistaken a simple gesture of affection for something else. Yet he did nothing.

Gramps continued, "We may need money, Loren, but if I had known the kind of job you were going to take—"

She kissed her grandfather warmly on the cheek. "I don't know why you're so upset. I only kiss them in the morning before their shifts start," she said innocently. "It's in my job description: 'Develop through one's own initiative a variety of programs to motivate employees.' Production is definitely up—"

Bill threw up his hands. "Buck, I'm too darned old to take her over my knee. Why don't you try and wipe that smile off her face?"

"I think," Buck interjected dryly, "that Loren would like to show us her plant."

The tour took a half-hour, from the spotless tool room to the noisy roar of the production floor to shipping. They dodged forklifts, rolling carts of raw material, bins of finished product. Loren was suddenly very serious, knowledgeably discussing press capacities and parts' tolerances, enumerating all the phases of production beginning with the product designed at an engineer's drawing board and ending with the finished containers loaded on a semi-truck for shipping. She was stopped—the janitor had a picture of his new grandchild; the maintenance foreman had a problem with one of his electrical apprentices; a word had to be said to the press operator who broke the month's production record.

It was her turf, and she showed it off with pride. It was Gramps's arm she hung onto—and delighted at seeing him sober on a Friday afternoon—but it was Buck she was conscious of. His hand at the small of her back as they dodged machinery, his face close when she was trying to talk over the roar of the presses, the feel of his rough wool sweater and the muscle beneath it when she touched his arm, steering him in another direction. He fired off questions almost as if he cared, as if he knew something about raw materials and production schedules. Only occasionally did she see a flicker in his eyes that communicated the same physical awareness that felt to her like an assault . . . a very gentle assault. In his eyes, she saw respect, and she valued it.

"Well, what did you think?" Loren demanded as they again passed through the revolving doors to her office. "I wish I'd asked you to see the place before, Gramps. I never thought you'd be interested."

"Loren? I've been trying to catch you since lunch. I've got—"

Frank stood in the doorway, a sheaf of papers under his right arm, running his hand through the hair that wasn't there as he always did. He halted when he saw her two visitors.

"Frank, this is my grandfather, William Shephard. And a friend of ours, Buck . . . Smith," Loren improvised. "Gramps, Buck, this is my boss, Frank Humphreys."

Frank stepped into the office and shifted the papers to under his left arm to extend his right hand in greeting, first to Bill, then to Buck. There was a pleasant moment of simple chit-chat, and Loren watched, feeling oddly unsurprised to see Buck take over the conversation. Research was Frank's secret passion; Buck had ferreted it out within minutes, the two of them discussing future markets as if they were tennis pros discussing Adidas. Why wasn't she surprised? she wondered fleetingly. She didn't really know Buck, not his background, or anything about his family, not even his last name. Yet she couldn't help thinking that Buck would have been so much better than Frank at the helm of this company, that he would never allow himself to invest too much time and money in one arena, as Frank did . . .

Frank beamed at her as he moved to leave, then remembered the papers under his arm. "You take the rest of the afternoon off, honey. You've earned it. Take your group out to dinner, why don't you? But I was wondering if you wouldn't mind taking these home to look over on the weekend. I just haven't the time—"

"Of course." There was just a trace of irony in her voice. Frank never handed out roses in one hand without thorns in the other. Or had he forgotten she had two jobs on her plate for the next two weeks without having any "little extras" added to it?

"Is he a decent boss to work for?" her grandfather asked as the three of them went out to the parking lot.

"Since he lets me do just about anything I want, I have to say yes," Loren answered thoughtfully. "It wasn't that way at first. I think originally he hired me with a view toward speedily firing me. And he did fire me. About forty-seven times. For everything from wearing sandals in the plant to talking back to him. No one else does that." She paused. "Someone has to do it. Otherwise, he'd be all tied up in research, and he'd never see what else was going on."

"So you're bossy on the job as well as at home," her grandfather grunted.

"Sad but true," Loren teased, and hugged the old man. She glanced up at Buck to find his eyes gleaming with amusement. "Have I been showing off too much?"

He nodded, she chuckled. "Okay, where are you two gentlemen taking me out to dinner? And what are we driving in, by the way?"

They were driving in a very sleek dark green New Yorker, not exactly the obvious choice of vehicle for an out-of-work redhead. She told herself not to ask questions about something that didn't matter and slipped into the comfortable frontseat as Gramps settled in the back. It was a lovely restaurant they went to, one of the few better places in the city that still didn't offer liquor. She appreciated Buck all over again for his sensitivity, and though she had no illusions about an immediate permanent change in her grandfather's habits, he seemed to be coping all right for the afternoon. They talked sulky races and politics and weather and the way it used to be, all Gramps's topics, with Buck keeping the ball rolling nicely. He'd slipped next to her in the booth and had his arm around the back of it until dinner arrived, so that she had to touch him if she so much as breathed.

She breathed. He felt warm and solid, and every time she looked up at him to say something, she felt a little warmer and a little less solid herself, and a great deal more quiet. She found herself ravenous over dinner, and there wasn't a shadow of tension until it was over. It was bound to be a little awkward when she paid for the meal, but Buck, after all, was unemployed, and she felt she owed him anyway because he had spent his afternoon watching Gramps for her. A little awkward was one thing, but...

"Just put it away, Loren. I can handle it," Buck growled.

"Of course you can," she said smoothly, yet clearly skeptical. "But I need the practice—women *are* paying for their meals these days, you know. It's not anything to..."

When the waiter returned, she had both of her hands pinned beneath the table with the bills still in them, and when the waiter was gone with Buck's money, her wrists emerged white from his grip. "For heaven's sake," she muttered to him furiously as they headed out of the restaurant.

"And the last name is *not* Smith," he muttered back to her. "The game was all well and good, Loren, but it's past time it stopped."

They were home by seven. Angela, predictably on a Friday night, was out with David. Bill challenged Buck to a game of chess, and Loren puttered around the house doing the little clean-up jobs she always did when she came home— a few dishes, lamps turned on, coffee made.

When that was done, she settled on the couch with the cost studies Frank had given her, the monstrous heels finally off, legs up, ankles crossed. The two men were playing their game at a table a few feet from her, engrossed in kings and pawns. She could still get Frank's work done this evening... but she didn't.

Her eyes kept wandering to the profile of the man concentrating on the queen his hand was about to move. He was crouched on a low chair, his legs separated and his elbows resting on his knees as he viewed the chessboard. Under the soft lamplight, his hair was a burnished brown, its red hightlights muted, and there was a strong streak of silver near his temples. Small lines were etched around his eyes, deeper ones between his brows; he had a beak nose and a very strong profile. The only soft feature in his entire face was his mouth, which she remembered with sudden fleeting intensity had been *very* soft. She wondered about the two scars on his face; his eyebrow half-hid the small one on his forehead, but the crescent on his cheek . . .

Their eyes suddenly met, and his held a challenge, a question. She'd asked him not to come back, and he had. She tried to tell him with her eyes that she was grateful for Gramps, and no more, but instead her traitorous gaze told him that he was a compellingly sexual man, that she was afraid, that there was a mortifying tension between her thighs, that she was very, very glad he had come back . . .

She sat up and tucked her legs beneath her. When she glanced back, his small smile was gone, and he was still staring at her, the desire in his eyes frank, sober, silent.

"Checkmate," Gramps chortled. "And I do believe I've finally had enough. I never thought I could beat you after you slaughtered me the first game, Buck. You must not have had your mind on this one."

"Nonsense. You beat me fair and square," Buck answered easily, but his eyes were still on Loren.

"Well, I, for one, am going to bed. A good night, Loren . . ."

She rose to brush a soft kiss on her grandfather's wrinkled cheek. "I'll put away the chessboard, darling."

"But don't think I'm not going to talk to you again in the morning about that job of yours," he warned her gruffly.

Buck disappeared for a moment while Loren put away the chessboard, and when he came back, he stood leaning against the doorjamb.

"I owe you," she said hesitantly. "For Gramps today. I mean, for taking care—"

"I like Bill, Loren. But I didn't come here for him."

She nodded. "I know that. But it's still a cause for celebration." She took a breath and suddenly smiled. "Come on." She crooked a finger, insisting he follow her through the hall and kitchen to the stairs that led to the basement.

"We're going—where?" he demanded.

"To see Joan."

The basement had been partitioned into half a dozen rooms for storage. Loren switched on the naked lightbulbs she needed to see and finally opened the door to a room where she and Angela stored their summer clothes. She burrowed between hangers and fabrics and finally emerged with a dusty bottle of wine in her hand. "It's a Château Lafite Rothschild, left over from my parents' era. Gramps would never look in our clothes, you see. That's why . . ."

"You don't have to explain, Loren."

"I know. Not with you. You've got your Aunt Emma," she said quietly. "Well . . . bye, Joan," she added impishly. "A perfect housekeeper," she told him. "She sleeps incredibly soundly. Doesn't mind the damp . . ."

"Doesn't need a bed, not fussy about the furnishings, doesn't get in anyone's way . . ."

She chuckled, leading the way up the stairs with a soft swing of her skirt. "Buck, I haven't got wineglasses. I don't know where they're packed away anymore. I thought the look of them would remind Gramps—"

"Loren. Relax."

She turned startled eyes to him and then . . . relaxed. She'd been gushing like a teenager. It just . . . wasn't easy. She knew all about work, about responsibilities, about exhaustion. She knew how to relieve a portion of that with a sense of humor, but she knew disgracefully little about serving wine, about talking with a man who . . . wanted her. There'd been no time for that. But then, Buck knew all about her life; in his eyes, there was just a hint of exasperation that she'd thought she had to pretend . . .

"Would you like me to build a fire in the living room?" he asked.

"Oh . . . yes!" And then she frowned. "But I don't know about the flue, Buck. There's wood out back, but——"

"You haven't tried the chimney out this year?" he guessed. "Well, we'll test a little paper first."

So with paper and twigs, they built a crazy little fire that gave off more light than heat. The excellent wine was served in water glasses. Loren's skin took on a warm hue by the firelight, and with her legs tucked under her, she felt very tiny next to Buck's long, stretched-out legs. He'd taken off his sweater, opened the throat of his dark charcoal shirt. "You were so good with Gramps," she said softly as she sipped the wine. "Perhaps that's part of it, that so much of his life has changed and he has nothing he can *do* anymore, what with old friends dying around him and he himself not feeling vigorous enough for real activity."

"Your sister said you tried a sanitarium for a while."

"My sister's answer to everything is to make someone else take responsibility," Loren answered dryly. She took another sip of wine and rolled the dry flavor of it on her tongue. "It didn't work, and he wasn't happy, and that took the last of Gran's insurance money. There's never any problem except for his Fridays. The day just holds bad memories for him . . . perhaps too many memories," she brooded softly, and looked up. "Your Aunt Emma?"

He set his wine down on the marble hearth and then did the same with hers. Watching him, she shivered, almost anticipating the hand that suddenly reached out to span the few feet between them. She had the option to take the hand or not, of course; she had the option to say no again . . . She met his eyes for only a moment, a grave uncertainty in hers, and then took his hand. Easily, he drew her close, enfolding her between his legs with her back nestled against his chest. He handed her back her wine and took his own, brushing a soft kiss in her hair as he did so. "I have no Aunt Emma," he said gently.

"Oh."

"My last name is Leeds, not Smith."

"You were offended when I introduced you to Frank."

"Furious," he agreed dryly.

She tilted her head back, smiling at him, but the smile faded. "I never really meant it as a game, Buck. I meant it as a gift...that I really didn't care if you had a cent or a job or were white collar, blue collar, or whatever. Honestly, it hasn't mattered to me. Not when I first met you, and not now."

He hesitated. "Drink your wine, Loren."

She did, leaning back against him, watching the little play of fire spark and sizzle and finally die down. He finished his wine long before she did, and from behind her he started a slow massage with his fingers at the nape of her neck, at the spot that continually ached after a long day. His fingers were firm and sensual and gentle-strong, but it was the graze of his thighs on both sides of her that forced her eyes closed. It was a unique sensation, to feel on the brink of danger and totally cossetted at the same time. Perhaps it was even sweeter because she really didn't care who he was or want to know anything about his past; she knew all she needed to know about him to be helplessly aware that she was falling in love with him. He was interfering, and he refused to listen to what he didn't want to hear, and he was too damned good at divining what was really in her mind. It wasn't right or sane or reasonable...but the tender first shoots of loving were there, as real as fear and daylight and fever and spring.

He took the empty glass from her, and she shifted, waiting. He held her head against his arm for a moment, looking down quietly down at her, his fingers smoothing back a wisp of hair from her cheek, over and over. "I'm not sure, Buck," she admitted in a low voice.

"Your hands are trembling."

"It's been too long. I don't even remember..."

"We're not going that fast, Loren. There's nothing to be afraid of," he whispered next to her ear. His lips followed the whisper, brushing the petal-smooth skin of her cheek. Tentatively, her arm reached up, her fingers exploring the faded crescent scar near his jaw, the shape and texture of his face, and then splaying in his thick dark red hair. When his mouth finally came down on hers, she welcomed the grazing soft pressure, her tongue waiting for his. His arms closed around her like velvet. She was aware of every inch of him, as if the world had suddenly crystallized around the two of them: his thigh and heartbeat, the threaded pulse in his throat, the hard tension in his stomach, and the power of his arousal, blatant in spite of the layer of clothes. His giant form dwarfing hers suddenly caused an involuntary tremor of fear.

"Loren?" He laid her so gently on the carpet, half-reclining next to her, his palm warm at the ivory hollow of her throat. She gazed up at him with luminous eyes, both of her arms resting loosely around his neck, answering his unspoken question. Her whole body was left vulnerable to him. He waited until that little flutter of fear passed; she could feel his eyes compelling her to stay open for him, to hide nothing from him. His palm stroked over her breast, down to her waist, then along the smooth stretch of hip to her thigh. She could feel a curling inside like a spring tightening when his palm caressed the gossamer of her stocking; yet her legs moved instinctively to close together. The little denial appeared to mean nothing to him; he kept stroking her thigh, firmly enough to radiate heat, finally a consuming heat, insistent, demanding . . .

She tensed when his hand came back to her throat, urging her neck back so he could drink of her sweet mouth again. Crushed against him, Loren felt a longing begin to spiral with his kiss; the weight of him seemed strangely familiar to her soul, strangely . . . right. When he drew back up again, the room seemed darker, and his eyes seemed darker, and her lips felt bruised, possessed. Taken.

Slowly, his palm caressed her torso again, down to the waistband of her skirt. The buttons of her blouse loosened one by one, and in one smooth movement he had enfolded her to him to unclasp the back of her bra. He didn't touch. Instead, his fingers reached up to stroke and comb through her hair until she felt like crying; it was as though he was deliberately trying to torture her.

"Loren?"

She didn't want him to ask her permission. And how did he know? They were secrets she barely remembered herself, the places where she knew control would slip, where it mattered very much that she trusted him. His palm stroked down to her abdomen, and like a schoolgirl she covered it. No. She completely changed her mind. Just . . . no.

He didn't move. He was breathing above her, his eyes dark on hers. She knew he would stop. To say she didn't trust him when she knew all she had to say was no . . . Her hand lifted, rested on the nape of his neck, and she drew his mouth down to hers with a sweet moan of fever. When his palm started a kneading motion on her breast and she felt the soft flesh swelling for him, the blood rushed through her veins like wildfire. A potent rhythm surged from the base of her stomach, and her thigh rubbed against his erotically of its own volition.

He shifted, and his hands molded her hips, rocking her against him in the same rhythm. Her hands slipped beneath his shirt, raking down the firm slope of his back. She felt wild inside, frantic, too warm, too close to him, and not close enough . . . it was a physical pain, after the long years of denial. "So sweet," he murmured. "Lord, I want you, Loren. I never intended . . ."

She forgave him the lie. Perhaps he even believed he hadn't intended to go so far. She knew better and had known it from the start. They were old enough to know that a struck match meant flame, to recognize the potential for flame every time they looked at each other. "I need you," she murmured back. His mouth found hers again . . . and again, and again. She did need him, his strength and his warmth, his passion and his unique, fierce gentleness. It was nothing like it had ever been with Hal; she had never envisioned anything like this with any man. She teased as he did, her palm smoothing down his chest to his ribs, gliding over his hip to his lean, hard thighs. She felt the explosive pounding in his chest, heard his breath quicken . . . They were lost . . . or perhaps found.

Chapter

6

THE BACK DOOR slammed in some other universe. Loren couldn't have cared less. She felt a stinging little slap on her bottom that was intended to reverse that. Still, her lips lingered on his throat, her fingers still grazed inside of his thigh... He slapped again. *"Dammit,* Loren."

His eyes were glazed, and his voice was furious; those huge fingers of his fumbled impossibly with the buttons of her blouse. She refused to help, loving the look in his eyes, hating the interruption she knew was coming... but there was a rich promise in seeing the evidence of her own feminine powers. He was all but coming apart at the seams.

"Loren? I came home early. The movie was an absolute bomb. Listen, I... oh!"

Angela stopped dead with her hand in midair as if she had been just about to brush back her fluffy blond hair. Buck and Loren were sitting by the hearth, undeniably together, but by then all the buttons had been conquered. Loren was sitting on her bra and Buck was finishing his glass of wine in a single gulp.

"Well! I mean . . . I think I'll go upstairs to bed now," Angela said hastily. Her sassy smile clearly offended Buck.

He raised himself up with a scowl and grabbed for Loren's hand, nearly wrenching her arm from its socket as he pulled her up next to him. "I'm taking your sister out for a while," he said flatly to Angela. "Bill's sleeping, but you stick around."

"Sure."

Angela hastily disappeared, but Buck was still pulling Loren. He went first to the closet for her coat and his, stalked through the kitchen, grabbed the bottle of wine, corked it one-handed, buried it on the top shelf of a cupboard Bill Shephard couldn't see without a chair, and propelled them both into the freezing-cold night before he released her aching wrist long enough to allow them both to put on their coats.

"Do you know how old I am?" he demanded harshly, but she could see the good humor beginning to return to his eyes as he reached down, gruffly shoving her hands away so he could button her coat himself. "It's your fault, dammit. I never did intend for anything to go that far, not in your house. I like *privacy*. Do you have any idea how long it's been since I've been caught in a compromising position?"

"How long?" she asked obediently, trying not to laugh.

"Never." He buttoned his coat then and grabbed for her arm as if he thought she were about to protest against going with him. But she wasn't. "I'm not going to touch you," he promised her rigidly. "I just want you to *myself* for a while. Any objections?"

"You're beginning to hurt my wrist," she said mildly.

So he released her wrist, opened the car door, and urged her in much more gently, locking her side as if he were still afraid she was planning a getaway. When he got in on his side, he fumbled for the ignition key and started the engine promptly. "I'll take you home whenever you want to go, you know."

"We seem to be having a rather major argument here. The problem is that only one of us is arguing," she said dryly.

He drew in his breath, and suddenly the corners of his mouth lifted. He put the car in gear and raised his arm to the side so that he could see to back up; his fingers reached out to tug at her rusty hair. "You weren't a hell of a lot of help," he said gruffly. "Somehow I was having a difficult time getting your attention. If you were counting on me to have all the control . . ."

"I was."

"Well, *don't*."

"I certainly won't," she agreed, her tone so irreverent that he glanced at her again and finally chuckled. His hand snaked down and covered hers, and they drove a while in silence. Loren was suddenly very tired, and it felt good to rest back against the seat with her head back, her hand nestled in his, the night all around them.

"Are you really so sure?" he asked her finally.

She smiled, her eyes half-closed. "Buck, I'm scared out of my mind. I don't give love easily—surely you've figured that out by now?"

"Loren . . ."

She rested her cheek on his chest. "Take me where you live," she murmured sleepily. "I've already half-pictured it in my mind. A one-man apartment, a very big bed and a very small kitchen . . ." She didn't notice him begin to stiffen beside her as she lazily described the kind of place she thought he must live in. Sensitive to his pride, she made a point of downplaying any image that connoted lack of wealth, or any negative reaction on her part to unmade beds or expectations of nothing beyond hamburger in the refrigerator.

Her eyes were closed when he made a u-turn; they'd stopped talking. She was still curled up next to him, trying desperately to talk herself into a state of wakefulness after a day that had begun at six. His chest was so warm, his collar soft against her forehead, and all the sexual vibrations lay quiescent in a lazy, somnolent feeling of anticipation, not to be hurried.

She didn't open her eyes until he stopped the car and then was shocked into wakefulness all too quickly. They were home—her home. And there was a strange almost-pallor beneath Buck's complexion in the dark, his jade eyes avoiding hers.

"What's wrong?" she asked softly.

"Everything. You're tired. I'm tired." He got out of the car and opened the door on her side. "I started to talk to you tonight and got sidetracked. Now all I've got in my damned head is making love to you."

Her eyebrows lifted. He sounded more than a little irritated about that. She shoved her hands in her coat pockets as she walked with him up to the house, shivering violently from the sudden cold after the warm car . . . and his warm body.

He turned the doorknob and pushed it open, but he didn't make any move to go in. Confused gray eyes turned up to his, waiting.

"Loren, I don't live where you think I do. There isn't a reason in hell for it to be any kind of a problem, but I think you're going to make it into one," he said gruffly.

She touched his sleeve. "Buck, I've tried every way I know to tell you that it couldn't possibly make any difference where you live. What you do—"

"Yes," he said crisply. "Just go in to bed; you're dead on your feet. We'll sort through it, Loren. It was a damned idiotic game we started to begin with."

Bewildered, she found herself on the warm side of the closed door, and alone. She stared out at the retreating car lights. Had she said something? Had he suddenly remembered a woman he had stashed at his place? More relevantly . . . was he coming back again? And wouldn't it really be better if he didn't . . . ?

She turned away, took off her coat, and headed up the stairs, thinking of the days ahead that would leave no time for a man, thinking of her life that simply had no room for

that kind of love. As much as she didn't want to admit it,
he'd hurt her with his abrupt withdrawal. A love affair with
a stranger, she thought wryly as she prepared for bed. Loren,
you knew better than that when you were fresh out of school.

It was still pitch-black outside, not yet six. Loren pulled
on a pair of well-worn brown cords that fit like a second
skin and then an old loose fisherman's sweater. The knee
socks, she noted sleepily, had holes in them. Furthermore,
one was black and one was brown. She debated momentarily
whether or not she cared. She glanced with sleep-laden eyes
at the distinctly solitary bed where thoughts of Buck had
kept her awake far too long into the night.

Wearing the mismatched socks, she tiptoed past Angela's
closed door, splashed cold water on her face in the bathroom, and ran a brush through her hair. Tiptoeing downstairs
in the darkness, she saw the thread of light beneath the
swinging door to the kitchen.

At the head of the table, Gramps was nursing a cup of
coffee. Loren bent to kiss him good morning, and he grunted
in response. They both liked their solitary six o'clocks.
Loren reached above the stove for a mug, then carried the
steaming cup of coffee with her to the opposite end of the
table. Her grandfather automatically handed her a section
of the newspaper, and she swung her legs on an adjoining
chair, crackling the paper as she decided against the front
page in favor of the feature section . . . which she didn't seem
to see.

Gramps looked old this morning, wearing a brooding
look like a second complexion, his hand shaky on his cup.
Most Saturday mornings he looked very much this way, yet
the hangover this morning was from life, not liquor. The
laugh lines in his face were more deeply indented than the
worry lines, and that told Loren a lot of what she already
knew about Bill Shephard. Laughter and an easygoing, careless charm that offered more than was delivered had been
his chief characteristics until the world had crashed all around
him. His specialty had been making promises he couldn't

keep, and he had hurt Loren as a child, had kept on hurting her until she developed a skin so tough that she no longer had to believe him to love him.

She sipped at the strong, bitter coffee, trying not to think of how the evening with Buck had ended. She thought instead about money.

Her paternal great-great-grandfather, with a third-grade education, had single-handedly amassed the original Shephard fortune—railroads, real estate, insurance, and farms. Making money had been an obsession with him, and he'd sold his soul in the process. Henry Shephard had been a miser, his family still living in near-poverty long after he'd bought his first bank. But Henry Shephard, Jr., the miser's heir, had changed all that. He, too, knew how to make money, but also how to spend it, and to him the Shephards owed the once-elegant home that Loren so loved.

Her grandfather was the only son in the family who'd survived Henry Junior. Bill had no business sense, though his dominating father had forced him into the family enterprises. By the time his father died, Bill had given up whatever other dreams he might have had. But he couldn't force himself to acquire business acumen, so he gambled on the side, and down slid the Shephard fortunes. Loren's Gran had died in a fall, though she would have lived with proper care—but no one found her for two days. Bill had made her promises, but those that he kept all had to do with money. Gran died alone, on a Friday.

Loren rose, refilled Gramps's cup and then her own, swinging back in her chair with a leg tucked under her. Her father, too, had had a preoccupation with money, as in spending it—the yacht, the Morgan, the cottage house, and tennis courts, and jewels... Loren had barely known the glittering couple whose death in a yachting accident had orphaned her. She remembered laughter and parties and swift good-night kisses... and a thousand promises given, never kept, ranging from a piggy-back ride to a trip to the Taj Mahal. Time and love were the promises broken: money always came first.

She'd met Hal after the empire had already collapsed, and she'd been going that same obsessional road. Hal had money; having lost all of her security, the twenty-year-old Loren had clung to him as to a life preserver. Had she realized how shallow he was, how lacking in character? If so, she'd been too foolish to care. He'd promised love, and he gave her his brand of it between cocktail parties, mostly in the middle of the night. She was shattered for a long time after leaving him. There was a tormenting guilt to deal with——for hurting a man who had really done nothing so terrible to her but live by his own values: that promises didn't mean anything, that money could compensate for love, respect, intimacy...

Bill Shephard suddenly cleared his throat. "Did he stay long last night?"

Loren blinked, folding the paper neatly. "No." She didn't pretend not to know whom he was talking about. "Want some breakfast, Gramps?"

"Oh, I'm not so hungry this morning."

"Scrambled eggs? French toast?" Loren coaxed. "How about pancakes?"

"Well, maybe..." He watched as she took out a bowl and started to put the ingredients together for pancakes. "Interesting man," he commented.

"Mmm." The batter was blended quickly, and then she bent down for the old iron griddle that had lasted for generations.

"Got a good head on his shoulders, that man. Good sense of humor. I never did trust a man who didn't know how to laugh." He paused. "There aren't many men around that you don't buffalo, Loren."

"How many pancakes did you say you could handle?" Loren asked as she popped small pats of butter onto the griddle and watched them sizzle.

"I hope you wouldn't be so damn foolish as to worry someone like me by sacrificing a chance for your own happiness."

"I'm making them nice and thin the way you like them,

and I've got enough batter here for a hundred." Loren bent down, kissed his forehead, and said affectionately, "Shut up, Gramps."

She was turning from the stove with a fresh plate of pancakes in her hand when she saw Buck's face in the glass window of the door. The sun was just peaking over the horizon behind him, a watery, lemony early March sun; his hair looked burnished in the weak light. His shoulders were huge in a dark olive jacket, and he was looking straight at her, a look that very much echoed the earlier part of yesterday evening.

She put the plate on the table and her hands on her hips, her silvery eyes echoing the end of the last evening.

He turned the knob and stepped in. "Mr. Shephard . . . good morning."

Gramps turned and stood up in surprise, a welcoming smile wreathing his features. "Well, come on in, Buck," he said jovially. "We've got pancakes for a hundred; Loren just said it. I can't say I expected anyone else to be up at this hour. Loren and I are both early birds . . ."

"I gave up sleeping myself about two hours ago," Buck responded. He was just unbuttoning his coat as he descended on Loren. His eyes glinted with determination. "I have to admit I'm starving." He tilted up her chin and planted a kiss on her mouth before she could protest. "I want Loren for the day, Mr. Shephard." But he said it directly to her. And then he turned away, reaching for a mug as if he owned the kitchen, and carted the steaming cup over to Gramps as he sat down. "She's going to raise a pile of objections. All the chores she has to do on a Saturday . . ."

"Nonsense!" Gramps rose like a trout for a favorite fly. "She's been working too hard as it is, thinks we can't get along without her for a day. The fact is, her sister could lift a finger once in a while—"

"Pancakes are burning," Buck murmured to Loren.

She whirled. Down the drain, four pancakes . . . Oh, well, there were plenty left. Buck devoured sixteen, one after the other, all the while charming Gramps without another word to her. She marveled, considered sending him packing, considered how all that arrogance made her want to laugh, considered how good he looked in that rough wool shirt . . .

"Well." Buck rose, patting his flat abdomen, which didn't look in the least filled. The jeans were molded to his long, lanky thighs; she could have put both of her feet in one of his walking boots. He reached for the olive jacket. "Get your coat, Loren—"

It was exasperating having to look up damn near a foot. "As soon as I do the dishes," she said firmly. Giant or no, he wasn't going to push her around.

"Don't be silly," Gramps intervened. "And Angela'll get the groceries today, Loren, so don't be worrying about that. You think the two of us can't put together a sandwich? You just go off and have a good time."

Buck was impatiently holding her jacket, his own already on.

"Well, I certainly am going to change clothes—"

"No, you don't. I've already noticed that your socks don't match—and you don't need makeup. It's just not going to be that kind of day," he said impatiently.

Outside it was fresh, cold, and glistening. Lacy patterns of frost covered rooftops and windows, and Loren could see her breath take form as steam. When Buck turned from closing the door, he just looked at her. His eyes were the only warm things on that cold, silent morning. Warm. And private. His thoughts were clearly X-rated.

She bit her lip. "Do you always blow hot and cold over the period of a few hours?" she asked conversationally.

He sauntered down the steps. "If that's a reference to the idiotic way I left you last night—"

"It is," she agreed.

He opened the car door, and she slipped in. "I had a feeling you were going to take exception to my Van Goghs if I took you home last night." He closed her door and went around to his side.

"I was not expecting *Van Gogh*," she said heatedly when he settled in beside her and started the engine.

"Yes," he agreed. "We're going to get it all straightened out today, half-pint. Consider yourself kidnapped." He motioned to a small bag between the seats and urged her to open it. "I feed my kidnap victims. I wasn't expecting breakfast, Loren, but I know darn well you forgot about it for yourself."

They were the kind of powdered-sugar doughnuts that left a trail of sweet white flecks on her chin and lips, and he chuckled every time he glanced at her. At the first red light, he leaned over to take care of one sticky spot, the wickedly smooth curl of his tongue on her cheek sending a shiver down her spine.

She didn't understand him, but it was difficult to keep up a sensible wall of defenses when he was so easy to be with, when he made it so obvious he was glad she was with him. As the miles disappeared with the doughnuts, she slid comfortably down in the seat, took off her boots, and curled up her knees. She felt a little like a gambler on a roll who could lose it all but just couldn't bring himself to get up from the table yet.

"How can you *sit* like that?" he said incredulously. "You could probably tuck up and fit inside a basketball."

She raised her eyebrows at him expressively. "I should have guessed from your height that basketball would be your game. I suppose that's another less than subtle reference to my size," she added dryly. "There are an awful lot of advantages to being small. Bath towels go a long way. Jeans are cheaper in the children's section. Half-price at the movies if I put a bow in my hair. I still get a sucker at the bank . . ."

"Does the sass come with the size, too?" he asked.

"I do believe that comes in all sizes " she said pointedly.

He had a wonderful laugh, free-flowing and husky. "We're going to have a fine day, Loren. You curl up any which way you want; we'll be there in another twenty minutes."

Chapter

7

THE LAST PART of the ride was through a densely wooded area, on a dirt road rutted in places by melted snow. At the end of it, like a sudden surprise, was a cottage with a huge diamond-shaped lake in front of it. Bits of ice that had resisted the last thaw still floated, silvery and charcoal in spots as the wind rippled over the lake's surface. Dozens of other summer cottages populated the shores, but none of the others appeared inhabited—at least at this time of year.

Loren was restlessly shifting in the seat as Buck pulled up to the cottage. Before he'd turned the key, she had her hand on the door, but he reached over to grab her wrist. Her exuberant grin wasn't daunted by the strangely pensive look in his eyes.

"Loren, I brought you here because I knew we could talk without being interrupted. Look, it's just a cottage..."

"Just a cottage!" She all but burst out of the car and ran helter-skelter for the water. "Why didn't you *tell* me you lived on a lake? What on earth was all the fuss about last night?" she scolded excitedly. "Have you got a rowboat, Buck?"

He sighed, following her. "I don't suppose you want to hear I have a Crisscraft power boat."

"A rowboat's all we need."

He sighed again. "Loren, I had in mind appealing to your rational, down-to-earth, practical little self today. I want you to listen to me—"

"Certainly!"

He watched her race to the water and shout complainingly when her fingers were chilled by the icy temperature, the hood of her jacket leaping back to put sunlight in the chestnut of her hair. Her eyes sparkled back to him, the child in her for once let loose as she raced down the sandy shore with her arms outflung, embracing the wind.

"Would you come back here? You're going to freeze that little fanny of yours right off!"

When she returned to him, her breasts were rising and falling in quick little breaths, and there was pure mischief in the grin she gave him. "Go away," she ordered him saucily. "Come back and get me in a couple of months. I haven't spent any time near the water since I was ten years old!"

"Which is about what you look." She didn't, though. It was distinctly a woman's curl of bottom and thigh in her tight jeans, a woman's way of moving, a woman's delicate profile of high cheekbone and slim little nose. Her lips were red and moist, and there was high color in her cheeks from her run, but she darted ahead of him, sensing he was going to grab her.

"Oh, no, you don't," she said teasingly. "Get your mind out of the gutter, Mr. Leeds. I want to see the inside."

"I was just going to warm you up."

"I'll bet you were!"

Digging a small key from his back pocket, he held it out in front of her. "If you want to get inside . . ."

"Bribery? In that case . . ." She stood on tiptoe and brushed a kiss across his mouth, shivering at the sudden look in his eyes, her fingers lingering on his neck. Her spirits were suddenly not dampened so much as softened; a gemlike flame of exhilaration had been ignited within her and glowed brightly. She rocked back down from her tiptoes, feeling warmth in her cheeks, an odd shyness.

"So it's occurred to you, too?" he said wickedly.

"What?"

"That we can't kiss very well standing up. There's too much difference in heights."

She wasn't ready to make the obvious comeback, that they could kiss very well lying down. "Let me in," she ordered sternly. "You're just trying to keep me from seeing what it looks like."

When he opened the door, she stepped into a small rectangular kitchen. A little wooden table with two chairs, a refrigerator and stove that had seen a quarter of a century, and—shock of all shocks—a claw-footed bathtub. The firstdoor she opened told her why. The bathroom had obviously been a late addition, and contained . . . a toilet. Nothing else, barely head room.

She slipped off her wet, sandy boots, absently handing her coat to Buck as she walked through the kitchen. There was only one main room beyond the kitchen, long and completely windowed at waist height for a complete view of the lake. There was a fireplace and a woodstove, logs stacked neatly on both raised brick hearths. "The fireplace in itself wasn't enough to heat the place," he explained, "but by the time I get the woodstove going, it'll be warm everywhere but upstairs."

The plush shag carpet was a mint-leaf green. The luxury of it momentarily disconcerted Loren, but there was very little furniture. An old rolltop desk, a pile of huge pillows on the floor, a pair of easy chairs with a low table between them, and a bookshelf filled with almost everything but books—a chess set, fishing rod, lantern. It . . . pleased her.

"I like it, Buck," she said quietly, turning to him.

"I was afraid you were going to say that."

She blinked at his ironic tone, but didn't really pay any attention. "You said there was an upstairs?"

She found it on her own, a little eaved loft without carpet, a double bed with someone's grandmother's quilt on it, an ancient antique dresser with heavy scrolls. It was freezing up there, but still she lingered, picturing it in summer with a cool lake breeze from the windows, picturing Buck sleeping there.

When she came back down, he was crouched by the woodstove, feeding it logs, and Loren watched for a moment. He knew what he was doing. He always seemed to know what he was doing. The confidence he exuded wasn't ostentatious; it was just there. She couldn't pinpoint why she felt so completely comfortable around him, but that was there, too; there was no need to hide her excitement over the lake, no cause for embarrassment about her mismatched socks. She wandered back into the kitchen.

"What are you doing?" he asked a few minutes later. He was leaning against the doorway, shaking his head at her quick movements in the kitchen.

"I can't just sit. Not yet," she answered frankly.

The groceries he'd brought had been put away, telling her that he'd planned on staying past dinner; inside the refrigerator there were steaks, a small bag of potatoes, and a bottle of wine. In the cupboards, she'd found self-rising bread flour, and her hands were already covered with it, her fingers kneading dough in the big bowl she'd found under the sink. "What on earth are you doing with flour like this? You surely don't make your own bread?"

"My mother does. She stocks the kitchen for me every fall. There are about a dozen containers of spices I still haven't figured out yet..."

She chuckled. "Well, I saw that woodstove and thought it would make a perfect spot for rising dough. It'll only take a few minutes. I put some water on the stove for coffee."

"I've never seen you move in less than double time," he

complained. "I had in mind watching you relax for the day."

"I *am* relaxed."

"That's what worries me."

She started laughing and couldn't seem to stop. It wasn't that she'd forgotten Gramps or Angela or the work waiting for her at home, but it had simply been so long since she'd had a whole day she could call free. That bubble of freedom seemed to act like yeast in her system, laughter close to the surface every moment, joy in the silliest things . . . She made Buck knead the dough, laughing at the pained expression on his face as his big hands coated with the flour mix. While the bread was rising on top of the woodstove, the two of them were picnicking beneath it, munching on peanut-butter sandwiches as if they were gourmet fare. A quick cleanup and they were outside, setting off to walk the entire circumference of the lake while Buck regaled her with the personalities of the cottage owners.

"Mrs. Bradford, she screams bloody murder at the sight of a garter snake, but makes brownies for the summer crowd . . . Horace, he wears an old Hawaiian kind of bathing suit that goes down to his knees and, by God, they're bony. He's at least a hundred and ten, an old recluse . . . the Redfords, they can't swim. I haven't figured out yet why they wanted to live by a lake . . . Brown's got two teen-age daughters and sits out on his porch every evening with a shotgun in his lap. God forbid anybody should look at his girls . . . Elizabeth, her place looks like she even dusts the grass, her flowers wouldn't dare wilt . . ."

He was crazy, absolutely crazy, hauling her up like a sack of potatoes when she made the slightest mention of weary feet—and it *was* a long haul around the lake. Toward the end was a race that Loren won, having started with a two-hundred-yard advantage in a two-hundred-fifty-yard dash. She taunted him with her victory the rest of the way home, tucked under his shoulder for warmth, but when they finally reached the cottage, everything was frozen from her toes to her forehead. They were both exhausted, a matched pair of disheveled redheads with pink noses, in stockinged feet, arguing over the position closest to the woodstove.

"Have I *finally* worn you out?" Buck demanded as he brought in mugs of hot cider from the kitchen, with cinnamon bark for swizzle sticks.

Loren nodded, taking the cup with both hands to warm her fingers. She felt a lovely kind of tiredness, her legs just pleasantly aching from the long exercise, the frantic pressures of her normal life relegated to some other world. She felt deliciously lazy; it was so cozily warm, and the room was scented with the sweetish cherry-wood scent given off by the stove. She sipped at the mulled beverage, her knees drawn up, her toes curling as the cider seemed to curl deep inside of her. "Tired . . . and disgracefully happy," she admitted impishly.

"Nap time."

He dropped two of the floor cushions a few feet from the woodstove, took the empty mug from her hand, and nudged her stomach with one of his big stockinged feet until she obediently lay back, laughing. From the closet, he drew out a handmade quilt like the one on the bed upstairs, not a heavy thing but a soft, lightweight covering. He covered them both and then lurched up again to lean over her reclining form, pulling off first her socks, then his. "Can't sleep with feet covered. No one can sleep with feet covered," he informed her gravely.

"And to think I never knew that," Loren said, according proper respect to the Oracle at Delphi.

He grinned, rolled her over to her side, curled her back to his chest, and closed his eyes. To Loren's total amazement, her eyes closed, too.

It was just a little cooler in the room when her eyes flew open. A watery sunlight beamed late-afternoon rays onto her hair, and when she half-turned, she found Buck stretched out next to her, leaning on one elbow, watching her with heavy, hooded eyes.

They had touched a hundred times that day, but not in passion. It mattered to Loren that he had waited, had first created a feeling of closeness and empathy that had nothing to do with sex. She knew it was coming, but she hadn't known he would find a way to make it easier for her, so that the transition to intimacy felt natural, simple... inevitable.

She felt a sleepy glow from within at the sight of the need in his eyes and reached up to touch the unsmiling features of his face, the crescent-shaped scar at his jaw. His head moved, pressing a kiss to the inside of her wrist. "May I take off your sweater?" he murmured.

She shook her head, just a little. She would do it, and she wanted him to know that, yet she found her fingers fumbling a little. The wool sweater was bulky and completely concealing; there was a strange shyness in daylight, a faint fear she would not please. When she had pulled the garment over her head, she sat very still in that little circle of sunlight, her hands trembling just a little. She met his watchful eyes, needing to see herself the way he saw her.

She was afraid she was too thin. Her neck was too long, her shoulders too pronounced... yet that wasn't what his eyes reflected back at her. Her soft skin was sleep-flushed, warm. A faint shadow divided her breasts, the swell of silken skin more pronounced on one side than the other because of the way she was sitting. The delicate lines of her collarbones, the wisp of mauve lace she called a bra, the hollow of her throat... In his eyes, she saw herself as lovely, cherished; just by looking at her that way, he seemed to claim every plane and hollow and curve. For a long moment, he didn't even touch.

"Buck..."

Her hand reached for him, and he caught it, held it. "I love you, Loren. I never had any intention of falling in love with you..."

It was so much more than she expected to hear, and her own emotions brimmed over in response. The shyness left her, the caution of years, the old images of herself. She unclasped the bra with her eyes lowered, then slipped slowly from the jeans. She wasn't finished before he'd urged her back to their deep carpet mattress, his mouth hungrily on hers as she kicked off the last of the corduroy fabric from her ankles. And then she molded herself to him, bending to his weight and warmth, her skin supple and giving for him.

She had never cared enough to really know a man's body. She craved the knowledge of his. The exact way flesh covered rib, the patterns of the hair that matted his chest, the feel of his skin, the scent of it. She explored first with her hands and then with her lips, pushing aside the shirt she had unbuttoned, every sense exploring him with intense concentration.

She heard a guttural sound of pleasure in his throat and slowly stretched down the length of him. Her nipples flattened against his bare chest; their heartbeats meshed and echoed one another; a more primal rhythm stirred inside her. Her thighs and stomach felt extraordinarily soft next to the stiff denim of his jeans; she rimmed the waistband of his pants with her fingers. For all the size of him, his waist was narrow, his buttocks flat. Her fingers splayed, learning boldness, indenting his bare skin through the fabric while his palms slipped beneath the lace that covered her hips, drawing her close, defining the exact measure of his arousal between them.

She knew he could feel her quickening, the way her thighs suddenly tightened, the way her breasts swelled against him. Yet her restlessness slowed rather than hurried him. His tongue flicked at her breasts, tasting the hard pebble of one nipple, then the other, his hand molding the orbs of flesh erect for him. A sweet, slow rush started in her veins . . . and never stopped. His touch was tender and teasing and endless, as if he'd known her forever, as if his only goal was to savor her soft skin, the flat little curve of her stomach, the perfect cream of her thigh.

He drew down the wispy panties and finally stood up to take off his jeans, his other clothing. His eyes never left hers; she was trembling with the sudden separation, her own eyes like dark silver.

Her blood seemed to still for that moment he stood towering over her, before he came down to her again. She had
never felt quite so small, so vulnerable. In his clothes, Buck
gave the illusion of power, of strength; without them, his
flesh took on the truth of those characteristics. A blend of
the most primitive emotions seemed to swamp her mind as
he slid down next to her again, as she saw the fierce, dark
need in his eyes, as he drew her close once more.

Tremors shook her body at the sudden total awareness
of intimacy. Like shock waves, the graze of his bare, hard
thighs against her own, the feel of those thighs against the
smooth palms of her small hands. She could feel the building
tension in his every muscle, and her hands courted those
shock waves, danced with danger. He shifted slightly, and
she shifted with him. The thought of any further separation
was intolerable. As if he understood, his mouth captured
hers yet again, his tongue-play increasingly erotic, and she
returned a pressure equally explosive as she learned what
pleased him. She wanted desperately to share in a way she
had never understood sharing before. Her palm glided over
his hip to his abdomen to more intimate flesh. He stopped
moving, and a shudder took his body, then his lips softened
on hers, their pressure suddenly tender. "Loren. You're so
small. If I hurt you . . ."

"You couldn't," she whispered back. So sure. Rationally, perhaps she was not so sure, but her emotional instincts
already had the answers. He was impossibly tender for a
man of such physical power and size; his touch had more
giving than taking.

"My sweet lover," he murmured as he took her lips
again . . . and again. Her throat released little erratic sounds;
a silken sheen of moisture was beginning to coat both their
skins. His hand stroked the length of her over and over,
each time teasing closer to the feminine core of her. Her
nails dented his back when he touched, invaded
. . . "Please," she murmured helplessly.

Her skin was on fire; the dark desire in his expression
pulsing through her bloodstream. She could feel restless

tears in her eyes when he moved over her, soothing her with soft love words, and then he was within, filling her to her soul. The silken seduction was completed; neither of them wanted to dally any longer. It was a fierce climb up, a splintering of the senses, a wild, uncontrollable feeling of soaring. Explosive shudders echoed over and over in Loren's body, she heard Buck's hoarse cry.

He held her cheek to his chest for a long time afterward. Loren felt drained, even bewildered by the explosiveness released in her own body. Buck kept stroking, stroking . . . until her breathing became normal, until she became conscious again. The fire was sputtering in the stove, the daylight fading rapidly; there was a soft quilt beneath her.

"That was a mistake, you know." Buck's palm lingered on her throat, then arched her neck back so he could see her face. Sleepy and flushed, her features seemed different after lovemaking, and the look in his eyes was possessive, taking in the unique and intimate loveliness that he had brought out in her. "Definitely a mistake," he growled. "You just lost the option to back out, Loren. I'll never let anyone else touch you."

She half-smiled, shaking her head just slightly at his nonsense, still bemused by his loving. He kissed her forehead gently. "You love me, little one."

"I love you," she agreed. It wasn't hard.

"I don't know how you managed celibacy for all this time, Loren, but you certainly weren't cut out to be a nun." He shifted, sitting up to draw on his shirt, clearly amused at the sudden color in her cheeks. "In fact, it doesn't make sense," he said gently. "Did that ex-husband of yours leave scars, or have you still been caring for him all this time?"

He got up, motioned her sternly to stay on the floor as he put on his jeans. He went into the kitchen but returned just moments later with two glasses of dark red wine. She accepted hers, taking just a short sip, wanting very much to give him an honest answer to his question without quite knowing what to say. It had been important to her in her marriage that she please Hal sexually, and from his responses, she believed she had. But her own responses had been of a different nature, and until now she had always seen herself as loving but not particularly passionate. She had needed no outlet for what she didn't believe she possessed, and she had always had dozens of places where she could expend other kinds of love, from her family to her men at the plant...

"Loren? Is it memories?" he probed.

"No, nothing like that," she assured him finally. "It was more...just having to put some needs out of my mind, Buck. Responsibilities always interfered with forming certain relationships..."

"Yes," he murmured as he bent down to add wood to the stove. "We're about to talk about that, Loren. We're about to talk about a lot of things."

Chapter

8

THE BREAD WAS in the oven, the potatoes washed and jacketed in foil, and the salad made. Buck prepared the steaks. The dinner took twice as long to prepare because he kept stopping every few minutes to touch her. He had brushed her hair himself, had forced a pair of his socks over her derelict mismatches so her feet wouldn't be cold on the kitchen floor. She set the dishes on the coffee table in the living room because the kitchen was too cold, and by the time they sat on the carpet across from each other, Loren felt a permanent flush on her face. She had never felt quite so beautiful, so cherished, never so cossetted.

It had become dark outside, the way night pops down like a curtain in winter, and the lake outside was like ink, still and black. There were no other lights or signs of people around anywhere. They might just have been in a universe of their own making. The steaks steamed fragrantly, and butter was melting on the baked potatoes; she could not remember a dinner that looked or smelled as good. She was ravenous, and Buck served her a ridiculously large portion of steak—almost as large as his own.

"You *are* aware I'm half your size," she said teasingly.

"I'm aware of every inch of you," he scolded back wickedly, and then his smile faded, and he poured her a little more wine. "You really haven't given me much choice but to marry you, Loren."

She thought he was teasing. "Are you trying to spoil the first illicit thing I've ever done in my life?" Her smile disappeared when she saw his expression. "You can't possibly be serious!"

"So we haven't known each other very long." He took a bite of steak, his eyes boring straight into hers. "You know the core of the man, Loren. Well enough to have made love with him. Well enough to have said you love him. Have you changed your mind?"

She set down her knife and fork and curled up her knees, her hands in her lap. "Buck," she said despairingly.

"Did you lie, Loren?"

"No." She shook her head. "But that has nothing to do with it . . ." This tough, craggy-featured man had very soft eyes, at least where she was concerned. Or always had. But suddenly, those eyes took on an hard jade fire that seared, and the jaw set in lines that didn't give. She felt stunned, the world suddenly knocked for six.

"I know all about your family, and your responsibilities, Loren. We'll get to that. But we'll stay with the two of us for another minute or two." When he saw she wasn't eating, he speared a piece of steak and held it in front of her lips. He motioned to her twice before she took it. "I knew you weren't ideal affair material from the moment I set eyes on you. In fact, you're rotten affair material, Loren."

She found another tidbit of steak in front of her mouth before she'd finished swallowing the first. She swallowed, shook her head—but the fork stayed in front of her lips. "Buck . . ." Her parted lips were force-fed the steak; she glared at him.

"Apart from your character, half-pint, I'm not going to be satisfied with being squeezed into your busy schedule.

It wouldn't work, Loren, an affair. You said it yourself; you run yourself into the ground until there's nothing left over. There's no time for loving in your life. Or did you think you were just going to be able to walk away after today?"

She swallowed the steak and this time firmly pushed aside his hands. "No," she said quietly, "but I thought you would, Buck. I knew what I was risking when you came into my life. I knew my responsibilities and that I didn't have the . . . right . . . to a relationship. Love doesn't really conquer all; I'm not seventeen anymore. I wanted . . . my minutes with you, whatever we could have. But when I go home tonight, it's to Gramps and hiding bottles and Angela and the house. Then there's my job, the four-hundred-plus men, Frank, the extra paper work . . . I can't change that, Buck—"

"I can." He motioned to her plate. "Eat, Loren."

But she no longer felt hungry. Buck wasn't angry, but there was control with a capital C on his features, in the way his fork stabbed the steak, the way his eyes pinned hers, the way his jaw was set, and in the tension in his shoulders. Had she asked for so much? she wondered fleetingly. She had reached out to the one man who had touched her in so many years; was it so wrong to put everything aside on the promise of moments—when she didn't have any more than moments to offer?

He stood up, towering over her as he picked up their two plates. "Just stay sitting. I'll bring the coffee. I want you to listen—"

"Buck, I really think I'd better be going home," Loren said miserably.

He disappeared into the kitchen as if he hadn't heard her. She knew he had. Restlessly, she got up, stretching muscles suddenly taut with tension. She wandered to the bare panes of glass that overlooked the lake. A March wind was frothing up little silvery waves; clouds were ghosting across the night sky.

In the window's reflection, she saw Buck walk back into

the room, carting two cups of coffee to the little table and then standing, hands on hips, looking at her. She felt a sudden, mortifying awareness of the faint soreness she felt from his possession of her. She was his. Rationally, she knew better, but emotionally she was so conscious of that single physical truth that she felt the sudden blister of tears in her eyes.

"What matters is that I have you close," Buck said quietly, coming from behind her to pull her gently against his chest. At first her back was rigid and then not. It was a hug of warmth she could not deny herself. "That's all that matters, Loren. The only chance we have to build something together is if we have time together. That's easier than you know, but your pride is in the way, Loren—"

She half-turned to him, brushing wearily at her eyes. "Buck, I can't believe you're serious—"

"For a beginning, the name is Bartholomew Leeds," he said grimly. "Bartholomew Arthur Leeds. All the same, you call me anything but Buck and I'll have you over my knee with a hairbrush in two seconds flat."

He wanted her to smile, so she did.

"See this?" He pointed to the crescent-shaped scar near his jaw. "Where do you think I got it?"

"A fight," Loren guessed.

"A fall out of a tree when I was six. I don't tell anyone else that either," Buck said flatly. "The scar on my forehead was from a bike crash. The first actual fight I ever had was with a girl, and she won. I was eleven. It set my ego back years . . ."

Her eyes cleared with genuine amusement as she listened, both of them carting dishes to the kitchen. He had a reputation as too smart for his own good by the time he reached junior high school; since he looked tough, he played the part. He told a half-dozen tales where he came off as less than victorious; a swaggering Mr. Cool with the confidence of a wrinkled carrot was the image he projected to her, one she knew could not have been entirely true.

". . . There were six of them that talked me into it. I wasn't

even sure I knew what a red-light district was. I was only fourteen. The rest of the gang were sixteen or over—"

Loren wiped her hands on a dishtowel. "You didn't *really*
lose your virginity to a prostitute? I thought that only happened in books . . ."

"I don't think we'll dwell on that—"

"What did she look like? What did she do? Where was
it, Buck?"

He shook his head at her. "I would like to move past
fourteen, nosy; it was hardly the best of experiences. I
wouldn't even have brought it up, but I was trying to build
trust, Loren. To show you there is nothing I'm not willing
to tell you." He shook his head again with an amused grin
for her obvious fascination with the topic. "If you will let
me continue with this riveting saga—"

She poured fresh coffee for both of them and unplugged
the pot. "I wouldn't be a man for anything," she said
thoughtfully. "A fourteen-year-old boy having to prove himself . . . When I think of how horrendous it was to lose my
own virginity, and I was twenty and thought myself in
love—and a man is under so much onus to have all his
experience beforehand. We talk so much of women's lib,
when so little has changed for the men in our culture. It's
really not at all fair . . ."

"Well, now you've got me diverted." he said with mock
disgust. They both sat at the kitchen table with their coffee,
Loren with one leg curled under her, half-leaning against
the wall just as he was. "Horrendous, Loren? How did that
word just happen to slip out? You said it was your sex life
that kept your marriage together for as long as it did."

She'd forgotten telling him that. She stared into the dark
liquid of her coffee for several moments, all too aware that
certain truths did "slip out" when she was with him. When
she glanced back up to meet his eyes, she considered how
impossible it would be to lie to him. "It did keep us together,"
she said quietly. "From Hal's viewpoint. He wanted me,
and because of that . . . I stayed in the marriage longer than
I wanted to."

He, too, was silent for a moment, but his eyes never left her face. "And it was really because of that you stayed celibate for so long, wasn't it, Loren? Because you were afraid it would be an issue of having to pretend again with another man." His voice was low and filled with too much understanding; she stirred restlessly. "There's no pretending with us. There never will be."

"Buck—"

"I think it's damn near close to a miracle that no other man ever bridged your defenses. So much warmth, so much passion . . ." His tone hardened possessively. "Three days. A blood test, then three days."

Loren's head jerked up, and she set down her cup. "No."

"Are you going to listen?"

She sighed unhappily.

"The only job I was ever fired from," he growled, "was at Leeds Diecast. My uncle's company. I was seventeen, working there for the summer. I came to work in a black leather jacket, on a motorcycle, if you get my drift, and no one could get me to do anything so ordinary as punch a time card without my making a federal case out of it.

"My parents were both academics, professors at the University of Michigan. I must have gotten the brashness from my uncle. At any rate, he was a bachelor and the only one who ever volunteered to take me on. God knows where he got the patience. At least by the time I got out of college, a few of the sharp edges had been sanded off. Not much. He and I held World War III for a year. The next year, I started listening instead of talking. The third year, he retired, and six years ago I made the last payment on the business to him. It's mine, free and clear. In fact, it's double the size it was in John's reign, and I'm damn proud of it. Managing and marketing were the tricks—never mind. Since you just turned pale yellow, I know damned well you've got the drift."

He wrenched up from the chair and stalked to the living room, returning with his hand clenched around the neck of the wine bottle, glaring at her strained features. Two glasses clattered down from the cupboard, and he splashed wine into both. "I never intended to deceive you, Loren. The first time I saw you, I was in that bar to meet an old friend; it used to be a place to 'slum' when I was the kind of teenager I told you about. But every time I tried to tell you I wasn't on the unemployment line—"

"I understand," Loren said honestly. She had cut him off every time he tried to talk to her; it was rather insane. She had rushed in trying to be tactful, trying to assure him that his unemployed status didn't alter the essential respect she felt for him as a man. It seemed very funny suddenly. She picked up the wineglass and met his eyes over the ruby liquid. Every muscle in his body was taut, the green eyes aflame, the crescent scar oddly white with tension. "I feel rather foolish..."

"No, you don't. Your stomach's all tied up in knots because you know what's coming. Money *does* make a difference, Loren. We both know it."

"Of course it does," she agreed lightly. "We all prefer filet mignon to Hamburger Helper." She glanced at him again. "Buck, you're rather...intimidating when you're angry," she remarked absently.

"Come over here." He motioned her to his lap.

She shook her head.

Then he shook his and got up, moving over her like some menacing giant, his arms pinning hers to her sides. The lips that touched hers were petal-soft. Her throat arched back automatically, her eyes obediently closed. She took in all of him, the texture of his lips and his taste, the song of take-me already starting in her bloodstream. She felt the leashed control in his body...

When he leaned back up, he just looked at her. "You see," he said vibrantly. "You see, Loren. I'd like to offer you a nice indecent affair, but it just won't work. You've got your life all tied up in knots like a pretzel, and I won't settle for crumbs. As a marriage, however impetuous, I think it will work. I've never had the least urge to propose to another woman. You don't find love and the ability to live with someone—the desire to live and grow with someone—in everyone you meet. You're natural with me; I feel myself with you."

"Buck—"

"I want time with you. I want your energies. I want you next to me when I wake up in the morning, and I want you to *know* that you'll never have to go into that bar alone again. Your job—that's your business, your choices. The rest I can make *my* business with a ring on your finger, rights that don't come with an affair. Your house, Loren, repaired and restored. Your grandfather can have care if you want, companionship if you want. Angela can have the luxuries. The money is nothing to me, Loren, except that it will take the pressure off you—"

He stopped for breath, staring at her, studying her, and she lowered her eyes, taking a long draught of wine. "Perhaps you'd like to take me home now," she said brightly, and rose quickly from the table, then sat back down again, removing the thick pair of socks he'd given her to keep her feet warm. The holes in her own socks winked back at her; it wasn't as if everything she owned was threadbare, but the image was there. It really was so very funny . . . and all she could think of was the generations of Shephards who'd solved all their problems with money, who had solved none of their problems with money . . .

"No. I won't take you home."

She glanced back at Buck when she rose again, taking the wineglasses to the sink. He was dying for an argument; she had the feeling he wished she were a man he could take on with his fists. But she wasn't a man and she had no intention of arguing with him.

She washed the glasses, put them away, and left the room, bending to fold the handmade quilt on the floor. It had come from a closet, she remembered, but when she opened the closet door, the shelf was too high. Buck came from behind her, taking the quilt out of her hands, the look in his eyes a detailed reminder of what they'd done on that quilt. "Everything in its place? Now try to put on your coat,

Loren. Do it. See what happens."

She reached up, very swiftly, and kissed him. His cheeks felt rough from the hours without shaving, and her fingers lingered gently as she looked up at him with sad eyes. Every muscle in his body tensed, and then he jerked away from her, breathing heavily.

"Would you like to tell me why I have the impression you plan on never seeing me again?" he said furiously.

"Because that's the way it has to be," she said simply, and looked around vaguely for her coat. It wasn't in the living room or the closet. She'd given it to Buck when she came in. She retraced her steps to the kitchen, found it on a wall hook, and was putting one arm through a sleeve when he stormed in behind her.

"So you have some idiotic prejudice against money. Perhaps with reason. That doesn't change anything between the two of us. You didn't give a hoot in hell what I had or didn't have when we made love, now did you?"

"No," she agreed, buttoning her coat and slipping out of the back door to bring in her boots. The rush of freezing air brought a welcome numbness to her cheeks. "It matters now."

"Why? Exactly what has changed?" he demanded.

"Nothing yet." She watched him grab for his coat, almost flinching at the violent way he snatched for it. "But it would change, Buck. No one keeps me, and I won't play Galatea to your Pygmalion. I could see what was coming. You'd solve all my problems for me, would you? It's so damn easy when you have money—"

"A hell of a lot of your problems *would* be solved with money," he snarled.

"That's just it. It's like buying love. Like buying a perfect peach and watching it spoil. I know you don't understand, but I've seen all too much of it in my life." Her tone was rational and quiet. She sighed at his implacable expression, and then simply turned and walked out into the cold, feeling the salt sting of tears in her eyes.

The ground was uneven and slushy, barely lit by the

moonlight and stars. Through her tears, the ground looked silvery gray; the shadows of trees menacing. He was at the car door ahead of her, in time to see her in and slam it. When he slammed the door on his own side, the entire car shook. "So you're all done, just like that, Loren? How does it feel—a one-night stand? I got over liking that scene a long time ago, but maybe for you . . ."

It hurt; he'd meant it to. She didn't answer until they were out on the open road again, it took that long before the lump in her throat would dissolve. It took the same length of time for him to stop racing as if he were driving in the Daytona 500 and smooth the car down to a decent purr on the road. "I love you, Buck, and I loved our time together," she said finally, very, very softly.

"I wasn't talking about *buying* you, Loren. I was talking about lifting the burden of family and financial responsibilities from your shoulders. And *not* out of the 'goodness of my heart.' Out of selfishness. Because I want you to myself, time with you. If you can't see the difference between that and 'keeping' you . . ."

"It sounds good, but you're really talking about taking me over, Buck. The debt would just accumulate; you couldn't get out free and clear, and it would change how I felt about you. It wouldn't be freedom to love, but obligation, cluttering up whatever real emotion exists, destroying it. You don't know me well enough to be that sure you want a lifetime with me, Buck. But I know myself. I don't regret a minute of this afternoon, but I would. It would stop feeling like love and start feeling like an exchange—sex for money."

For forty minutes, they drove in silence, her last words echoing, leaving a bad taste in her own mouth. She could feel the first pangs of withdrawal stabbing through the numbness; he was withdrawing from her already, and he was next to her. She could still feel the imprint of his hands on her body, still feel the desire to curl close to him, still remember exactly what he looked like naked, leaning over her.

When he pulled into the driveway and stopped the car,

there was a cold, unreadable expression on his face. "You're a fool, Loren," he said in a low voice.

She took a breath to control the burning swell of tears just behind her eyelids and reached for the door.

He snatched her first, grasping at her shoulders to half-wrench her across his lap. Ignoring the shudder through her body, his fingers threaded roughly in her hair, molding her scalp to force her mouth to his. His lips meant to punish, and they did, with a savage pressure that bruised and cut where his teeth grazed against her soft flesh. As rough as he was, as raw, she could feel an eruption of sheer sexual desire rip through her, just as rough, just as raw. She felt an urge not to tame the primitive onslaught but to encourage it, to meet him on whatever ground he wanted to play. It wasn't Buck she was rejecting but his moneyed world.

He drew back from her, his hands clenched tightly on her shoulders, and then he pulled open his door. She could see his hands were trembling even more than her own. "I won't call you," he said harshly. "You call me, Loren, the next time you want a one-night stand. You want to give it away free and clear, with no strings attached . . . well, don't waste it on a stranger."

He stalked ahead of her to open the kitchen door. She walked up the stairs and then past him, too shaken to even look at him, and heard the door slam behind her. She was alone, a single light left on in the kitchen, the household obviously long asleep. She was "free and clear" to burst into tears, but the release was denied her, as if all her emotions had been buried in a dark box in her heart that had no key. A lump in the back of her throat was trying to choke her.

Her knees suddenly weak, she sat down at the kitchen table, cradling her head in her hands. She could not get over the horrifying feeling that she'd just made the worst mistake in her life and had no way to take it back.

Chapter

9

IT WAS PAST eight when Loren drove into her yard. With a weary sigh, she opened the back door of the van and reached in for an armload of papers to take into the house, hardly noticing the hint of crisp air that smelled distinctly springlike. The slush was long gone, and April only a few days away; a few trees were thinking about bursting into leaf, and the grass already had a lush softness of early spring.

Wielding her purse, folders, and keys, Loren slammed the van door with her hip and made her way to the kitchen door, wishing she had a free hand to rub the aching spot at the nape of her neck. In the dusk, there was no one to see her, and the total exhaustion etched on her features gave her a fragile appearance. Her workload had been impossible these last few weeks, even when she stayed late and brought work home, and she had launched a spring cleaning in the house as well. Every minute of every day had been filled, but there was a continual, aching awareness that Buck hadn't called and was not going to call. No matter how many times she convinced herself that she'd been both honest and right in what she'd told him, there was a lonely ache inside of her that just refused to lessen. Her weight had slipped five pounds, and unless there was a reason to make the effort, the ready smile and quick comeback she was famous for simply didn't happen.

Thinking of what to make for dinner and how to wedge in the paper work between the dishes and bed that night, Loren's step almost faltered on the stairs. She *had* to pull herself together, stop driving herself. She opened the door and promptly frowned as she set down the papers on the counter.

Every light was on in the kitchen, an unexpected and tantalizing aroma of beef stroganoff wafting from the stove. The counters were spotless; there were no dirty dishes waiting for her; the floor gleamed. More startling was the man standing at the stove with a wooden spoon in his hand. He was as small as her grandfather, but oddly spiffy in gray slacks and a starched white shirt, over which he wore a body apron. On the safer side of sixty, he sported a cane in one hand; he was stirring with the other. A pair of puppy-gentle eyes lifted to hers. "Miss Shephard?"

She nodded, not exactly sure what to say.

"I'll have dinner for you in about ten minutes. We've just been waiting for you to come in. I'm Rayburn, of course."

"I see." She didn't see at all, watching as he deftly handled the pair of pots on the stove. The puppy-gentle eyes spared her another shy smile.

"I can't tell you how grateful I am for the job," he offered warmly.

"The job," Loren repeated faintly.

"Your grandfather and sister are waiting for you in the dining room."

She resisted the urge to repeat that as well, instead removing her coat as she watched him, and finally giving in to his gently motioning hand to disappear into the other room. The dining room had been transformed; a white linen tablecloth graced with silver unearthed from locked drawers, not to mention the crystal and hand-painted china that were a legacy from past generations, a candelabrum in the center of the table . . . Gramps was in a suit and Angela in a low-cut red blouse; they were seated across from each other, all dressed up and like twin Cheshire cats.

"All right. What on earth is going on?" Loren said wearily.

Rayburn entered the room, again very gently motioning her to sit, his apron removed. She found herself sitting and then served as well, her plate heaped with asparagus in a marvelous cheese sauce, beef stroganoff, a tossed fresh spinach salad with a tangy dressing. Homemade bread was still steaming on the plate, cut in wedges. In her own glass, there was wine while the other two clearly held ice water, and again she looked up blankly at Rayburn, who stood patiently at her side. Something seemed to be expected of her.

"It looks wonderful," she said obediently. It wasn't hard to say, looking at the table.

"I love him!" Angela crowed when Rayburn returned beyond the closed door to the kitchen. "I just love him! He's so . . . butlerish. I can hardly wait to tell David. It's just like it used to be when Mother and Dad were alive!"

Gramps was looking at Loren. "Admit it's nice to come home and be able to relax for a few minutes, Loren," he said quietly. "Just eat your dinner while I explain."

When she'd walked in the door, she'd felt too tired to eat, much less cook, yet when she took the first bite, her appetite miraculously perked up, and she found the second and third bites going down while she listened. Jim Rayburn had a bad hip and consequently could not find work. An army pension was enough to keep him in adequate spending money, but would not in itself pay for living expenses. He had no family still living; after his discharge from the service, he had worked as a clerk, later as a cook. In exchange for a roof over his head, he was more than willing to both cook for the Shephards and do some basic housekeeping. "To take the load off you," Gramps finished.

"You look like hell lately," Angela added cheerfully.

"Thanks," Loren said dryly, and studied them both silently as they finished their dinner. The meal was superb, and to her own surprise she was finished before either of them, too sated to move. She felt relaxed and almost cheerful for the first time in weeks. Yes, it was wonderful not to come home to a load of housework and cooking. Yes, even those few minutes of being pampered soothed the taut nerves she normally came home with. Yes, she liked the idea of someone at home for both Gramps and Angela when she wasn't there. And yes, he was Gramps's age, perhaps company for those lonely Fridays... And she was not born yesterday. Neither Angela nor Gramps would meet her gaze. Suspiciously, she picked up the glass of wine and took a sip. "Where exactly did you find him? Are you going to try to tell me he just walked up to the door, looking for a job that doesn't pay, knowing all our circumstances?"

They were both silent, and then Gramps looked sternly at Angela, saying quietly, "We went looking for him. You needed help. You've needed it for an age. Since you don't have the sense God gave you to come in out of the rain, we found an umbrella for you."

"Thanks again," Loren said dryly. "In the meantime, how *exactly* did you find him?"

"An ad in the paper. How else would we find him?" Angela said swiftly. "In the meantime, Loren, I have other news, and since for the first time in a month you don't look like you'd like to snap my head off..."

"Angela!"

"I want you to go out to dinner on Saturday with David and me," Angela continued smoothly. "A dress-up, elegant dinner—all on David."

"Oh, Angie..." Loren's features softened even as a worried frown creased her forehead. Rayburn, her job, even Buck, for the first time in an age, fled from her mind. She could tell from her sister's face—from the defiance in her chin and the love sparkling in her eyes—what the dinner was for. "Honey..."

Angela shook her head. "I don't want to talk about it without David here. I know you think I'm too young, Loren—"

"Darling, it isn't just that. David isn't even out of school yet—"

Angela set her napkin on the table and stood up. "Loren, you had such a rotten marriage you don't even like to hear the word said. You hole up here in your little shell. That's not the way I want to live my life, and I'm of age. And I'll be out of school by the first of June."

She stalked from the room, and Loren stared at her grandfather as they both heard the rush of footsteps up the stairs to Angela's room, followed by the distant slam of the door. William Shephard stared back at Loren, and then he also rose. "Is that how you see me, too?" she asked helplessly.

He bent down to kiss her forehead before he passed. "Loren, you've been under pressure for so long. You're our mainstay, child; it's been so easy to take advantage of you. At the same time, you make it hard to show gratitude; there's less and less give and take in you, less ability to hear someone else's story. I dislike your sister's dramatics, Loren, but I can understand—she knows you wouldn't have been willing to listen to her if she had stayed. You listen to no one these days, as if you were the only one who could be right. Don't you really know better than that, sweetheart?"

He, too, left the room. Loren sat perfectly still, cupping her chin in her hands. For some odd reason, her heart was suddenly pounding, as if she were afraid. The silence and emptiness of the candlelit dining room hurt. *Was* she so rigid, was she unable to see another's point of view anymore? She thought not of her sister but of Buck, and love ached inside her like a needle-sharp pain, the loneliness suddenly unbearable. She believed what she'd told him, that his having money changed everything. She could never live off his bounty, could never take when she couldn't give in exactly equal return; she knew that his giving her *things* would eventually sour the kind of giving that really counted. She didn't believe she was wrong in what she'd done; it was only that being right seemed to have such a terrible price tag attached to it. Price tag. Money. Yes, she'd been right to dread the curse of it . . .

Rayburn brushed through the revolving kitchen door with a tray in his hand. There were three coffee cups on it, but seeing the emptied room, he poured only one, setting it in front of her, his soft eyes taking in her unhappy ones with a compassionate expression. "Sit down and have a cup with me?" she asked.

He nodded. "I thought you'd like to give me some instructions on the house."

She shook her head slowly. "Actually, I'd just like to talk with you," she said quietly. "I'm beginning to have the feeling I haven't really done that with anyone in a long time."

"Pardon, miss?"

She smiled absently at him. "I'm lonesome for company, and I'm beginning to have the feeling it's my own damn fault, Rayburn. Just talk with me, would you? Tell me about yourself . . ."

Angela stood in the doorway to Loren's bedroom. "You're *not* wearing *that*." She pointed to the beige suit laid out on the bed. Loren had a hairbrush in her hand and was standing at the window in a silky coral slip.

The suit was a severely tailored outfit, which Loren felt was appropriate for the dinner they were going to. It fit her well and made her look older, more responsible, and that was the role she knew she needed to play tonight with David and Angela. She opened her mouth to defend her choice and closed it again. "What would you like me to wear?" she said instead.

Angela looked startled at her sister's meek tone, but very quickly crossed the room to Loren's closet, burrowing for the better part of three minutes before she came back out again. "I want you to wear something *pretty*," she said belligerently. "You're always hiding your figure, Loren. We're going out to dinner and dancing, and I want David to see what you're like when you're having fun. Now this . . ."

Loren sighed. About a hundred years ago, she'd thought a black dress was the end-all of sophistication and chic. This particular "little number" had been shoveled to the back of her closet like a rabbit's foot, but it really wasn't her style. Nor did she feel she was going to be able to talk sense to the two younger people when she would worry every other minute whether inappropriate skin was showing. But perhaps if for once she seemed less like the Great Stone Face..."All right," she agreed.

Angela's eyes widened, and then she reached over to kiss her sister. "Good girl. We'll get you smiling yet, Lor. You just wait until you're glutted with lobster and champagne and soft music—"

"That's what you have in mind? Already I'm feeling like a third wheel," Loren said dryly.

"Is there a law against talking and having fun at the same time?" Angela demanded. "Now I'm going to come and check on you in a few minutes. *Don't* change your mind about the dress."

A half-hour later, Loren surveyed her image in a full-length mirror. Having decided to please her sister, she'd gone the whole way, but as to whether or not she pleased heself... The shoes she loved, a spangle of silver straps with high heels; the stockings were sheer and dark, like silk over the curves of shapely thigh and calves. And when she so much as breathed, the black chiffon skirt swirled around her knees in a sexy way that made her feel ultrafeminine,... but sexy should not be the operative mode, not for this dinner, she thought unhappily, and from the waist up...

The back was sheer chiffon, the same as naked, and the sheerness was repeated in the long, loose sleeves that banded tightly at the wrists. Except for a gentle drape of fabric across the breasts, the front of the dress was plain to a high-throated, stiff collar, and beneath was a lining so silky it was shiver material against her bare skin. The severe cut and color accented both her figure and her creamy skin, but Loren was uneasy—it wasn't so much the look of the dress as the feel of it. She felt...sinful. But Angela had insisted . . . Would Angie listen to a sister who didn't listen to her?

She might as well go whole hog. With a sigh, Loren brushed her russet hair back from her forehead, applied an eyeshadow called Smoky Sin and several coats of mascara. She was just reaching for perfume when she saw her sister in the doorway again, staring at her so intensely that Loren examined herself nervously in the mirror.

"Too much funereal black?" she questioned.

Angela shook her head. "Loren, I don't think you realize what a knockout you really are."

"No one who's five-one is a knockout, sweets." But she turned away from the mirror pleased and subjected her sister to an equally intense scrutiny. Angela was dressed in a mauve crepe top and pants, her blond hair swept up in loose curls on top of her head, and her voluptuous figure showed off to perfection. "Now you," Loren teased, "have got all the equipment to turn heads in any crowd."

David, with his shy charm, claimed they were both stunning. The restaurant was in Ann Arbor, a three-storied, open-balconied place called Blake's, where one could see all varieties of action no matter where one was located. The main door opened to a sing-along bar, the second story had pool tables, and the third a bass player providing quiet jazz from a candlelit corner. A live band playing disco was out of sight, and there was a bar on every floor. The clientele was young, a twenty-to-forty crowd with a mix of couples and singles.

David escorted them to the third-story open balcony with a view of two bars, a piano down below, and a quieter milieu than on the other floors. As promised, lobster and champagne were ordered, while Loren studied her sister's beau. Though far from handsome, David's angular, square face and husky frame conveyed a steadiness that had always appealed to Loren. His humor was shy, had to be coaxed out, but it was there. He'd been hooked on Angela from the first time he'd laid eyes on her, which had rather surprised Loren. The two were so different, David's seriousness to Angela's flightiness, his sense of responsibility to her devil-may-care insouciance. He gave in to Angela ninety-nine percent of the time; it was the one percent that Loren valued—David never gave an inch when it counted.

At home, she had deliberately not brought up the subject of marriage to Angela, certain the only response would be defiance and perceptive enough to understand that open opposition would only harden Angela's resolve. She ought to be congratulating herself that Angie was, of her own accord, thinking now of settling down. But she was too young, and so was David. Yet there had been an openness in Angela the last few days that Loren didn't want to spoil, a vulnerable pleading in her eyes when she looked at her older sister. Understand, for once, she seemed to be saying.

Thoughtfully, Loren waited through dinner, relaxing in spite of herself after the first glass of champagne. The food was excellent, and unconsciously she found her toe moving to the seductive jazz of the bass player in the corner. The tablecloths were blood red and the paneling dark; a single candle flickered on the table. Her skin glowed in the soft light, the flame sensuous and soft in her eyes. Her feelings showed in her expression, the real love and concern she felt for her sister, the haunted loneliness she felt watching the two of them very unobtrusively stealing looks at each other, a faint sensation of restlessness that the frankly sensuous dress she wore and the champagne and setting invoked. She wasn't lonely for company or even for an escort, but the image of a red-haired man kept intruding on her thoughts, a discordant note she couldn't seem to erase.

"Loren," David said gravely, once the waiter had served coffee, "I want to marry your sister."

She looked at him silently, cupping her hands beneath her chin.

"She can't cook," David said flatly. "She can't keep house, has never held a serious job, couldn't manage a dollar to save her life. On top of that, I'll be in school until December, and we want to be married in June. So if you think I don't know all the very good reasons why you're going to object—"

"David!" Angela interjected, protesting his picture of her unfitness to be his wife.

David flashed her an affectionate smile. "This is between your sister and me, angel." He leaned forward, his pale blue eyes on Loren. "I'm not going to stop loving her. You don't have to tell either of us that it'll be rough. She's eighteen and I'm twenty-one. We don't need your approval, Loren; we'd just like you to be with us. You know I'm working while I'm going to school, and my uncle's agreed to let us have the apartment above his garage. You know I'd never let her starve—"

"I didn't think you would. And I am—with you," Loren said gravely. "I only ask that you wait—"

"But we can't, Loren," David said with equal frankness.

"Why not?" Loren leaned forward. "David, the two of you have been open and aboveboard about . . . your closeness. Just a little more time, a little more maturity . . ."

"Lor, people get divorced at fifty. They're not *mature?*" Angela interjected. "Nobody gets guarantees. Nobody gets anything without reaching out and grabbing for it."

"This is our chance," David said quietly. "If we don't take it, it may be gone. Your sister could do all that 'maturing' with someone else, I could find someone else. You think I don't know that could happen? We take our chance, or it's gone. I don't want to risk losing Angela, Loren. So it's going to be tough, but that's what we want to go through together. Please try to understand."

Loren set down her empty coffee cup and sat back, fingering the nape of her neck restlessly. She felt a curious desire to cry. These two young adults were more romantic than rational; she'd seen so much more of life that she had dozens of arguments at the ready, all very good ones . . . But she heard them, really heard them: "Take the chance; there may only be one time . . ." She not only heard, she felt it suddenly in her soul; she felt it in the blue notes of the bass player and the single flicker of the candle on the table. How could she tell them they were wrong? She wasn't sure they were, not anymore, not when she'd turned down the only chance that meant anything to her, a choice that had ached inside her for weeks now . . .

And then she saw Buck, two floors below.

Chapter
10

"LOREN?"

Her attention flickered back to the young couple at the table. "I feel very strongly," she said quietly, "that it would be better for the two of you to wait, but as you said, David, you're both of age. I'll support whatever you both decide and help you any way I can..."

Angela let out a deep, heartfelt sigh and leaned over to kiss her sister. "Do you mind if we dance just one dance, Loren? There's a terrific band just out that back door on the first floor. We'd be right back."

Loren smiled at the two hopeful faces. "Of course not."

They left, arms around each other. Loren didn't see. Buck was below with two men, one of them an Afro-haired brunette with a mustache, the other light-complexioned, with hair the color of sand. The three men, drinks in front of them, were laughing at a round, crowded bar. Buck was wearing a sport coat, some soft fabric. Cashmere. Gray.

A waitress stopped before them; she was wearing a scanty yet lush uniform of scarlet satin designed to show off the upstairs she certainly had. The two men with Buck were attractive, thought Loren, indeed, more conventionally handsome than Buck was. Yet the waitress lingered by *him*, whispering something in his ear. He laughed. Loren could see his hand reach around to pat the satin-clad bottom. The woman was of a marvelously *normal* height, her seductive manner one Loren could never hope to emulate, and the invitation was clear when she bent toward him again, covering his hand to encourage familiarity.

You had *your* chance, you lost it, she told herself. But she found herself standing up, smoothing her hair with her fingers. Below, the waitress was walking away, Buck's eyes following the swing of her hips. The other two men were also watching her, and so, momentarily, did Loren. They were an expressive pair of hips. Clearly, an offer was being made. There wasn't a reason in hell why he shouldn't take it.

Loren's feet went into motion, following the red carpet down the circular flight of stairs to the second floor. There's no way you're going to do this, she told herself. But her feet kept moving, her heart pounding like a bass drum, a flush on her cheeks that darkened when a husky blond cruiser on the second level whistled a come-on to her.

On the first floor, the noise level was higher. From beyond closed doors, muted disco rhythms contrasted with an active piano bar; there was a steady hum of conversation over that, people entering and laughing as they shed their coats. Loren stopped in the middle of it, assailed by cigarette smoke, the whiff of alcohol, and a cool draught of midnight air from the constantly opening and closing door; all of the confusion made her shiver. She saw a man leering at her from behind a pair of wire-framed glasses, trying to catch her eye.

Buck was still talking to the two other men, standing around a semicircular bar along with other business types. He hadn't noticed her yet. All she had to do was go back upstairs; he'd never know. She would be the only one who knew there had been a second chance—and that she'd thrown it away.

Resolutely, she angled through the throng of people and tables until she reached him. Her palm tentatively touched the curve of his shoulder. Cat-aware, he whirled, his green eyes expressing fleeting surprise before they chilled over. His friends, interrupted in their conversation when Buck turned from them, were staring at her. The one with the Afro gave her an unobtrusive once-over, with a relaxed smile of appreciation and curiosity. The other man frowned momentarily at the interruption, and then continued to talk as if the others were still listening; he was obviously more than two sheets to the wind.

Buck's eyebrows lifted in question, but his eyes were clearly cold and unforgiving. She'd been written off; she could feel it in the pounding panic in her chest. "I saw you . . . and I thought I would say hello," Loren said awkwardly, her voice so low he had to bend to hear.

"Hello," he echoed back crisply.

The next few seconds seemed like several centuries. He noticed her dress and her figure, and there was an instant flare of something intimate in his eyes, but he was totally silent. They were not *friends*. He was not going to go through any social charades. Rage suddenly welled up inside Loren. *He* was the one who'd started all of it, who'd barged into her life in the first place, turned her head until she couldn't think straight.

Her poise had evidently been left on the third floor because she couldn't seem to think of a thing to say. He waited, still silent, for another few seconds, unsmiling, his soft gray cashmere jacket incongruous in contrast to the stronger textures of his brush-thick hair and leathery complexion. She had an urge to slap him. His silence taunted her, conveyed he knew well they'd said it all; that unless something had changed in *her* attitude, she might as well turn around and disappear again.

"You *did* tell me," she finally managed, in a deliberately

loud voice, "not to waste it on a stranger. That if I were lonely—"

His palm spun her around so fast she nearly tripped, seared by an iron brand on the shimmery chiffon material at her shoulders. He barked something rapidly to his friends even as he was pushing her away from their curious looks.

"Be very happy that no one in that crowd could conceivably have understood what you were talking about," he hissed harshly, stopping only when his friends and the other people in the bar room were out of sight. The dim entrance hall was lit by lanterns in sconces, and the air was cold from people opening and closing the doors.

"I didn't think you were going to give me any chance to talk privately," she responded calmly. "At least that got your attention." She felt almost sick inside, just from the touch of his hand on the nearly bare skin of her back; yet she also felt vibrant again for the first time in weeks.

"And do you have something you want to say—privately?" he said sarcastically.

"A public room is fine by me," she said cheerfully. "For that matter, if you'd rather I found someone else—"

The look he shot her sent acid to her stomach. It was the same feeling she'd had as a child when she'd changed her mind about the roller coaster ride after the first downward rush.

"Where's your coat?" he said tightly, his voice raspy.

She motioned to the third floor. He trailed her up the stairs like a bodyguard, trailed her back down again, into the black lights of the disco room to Angela and David, and back out again. The man on the first floor didn't leer this time, she noticed; nor did the bulky blond on the second floor. Buck radiated an aura of just-give-me-an-excuse-to-deck-someone. She couldn't understand why she was so thrilled to be with him again, but she was. Perhaps she was intoxicated with his aftershave, though the scent was neither woodsy nor musky, but just plain male. And she'd forgotten just how much she loved the odd green and the shape of his eyes, the way the wind tossed up his hair once they were outside.

"No wonder you're shivering in a dress like that," he snapped when they'd walked the half-block to his car.

"You don't like it?" she questioned.

He stalked around and closed the door on his side before answering, rising up in the driver's seat to fish for the car key in his pants pocket. "If I'd known what the back of your dress looked like, you'd have been backing away from the men in that bar."

She stared at him, half-smiling, as he drove onto the expressway. "You still haven't said if you like it," she murmured demurely.

"No. I *hate* it."

Carefully averting her face to the window, Loren smiled more broadly, glad her sister had forced her to wear the dress. She slipped out of her sandals and curled her toes toward the blast of heat beneath the console. She was as sure of Buck as she was of a caged tiger, but anger was not the same as rejection. If he didn't want her with him, she wouldn't be here.

"Your friend with the curly hair, was that the one you went to school with? The one you went to the Slippery Lady to meet?" she asked idly.

"I'm in no mood for chitchat, Loren."

So she was silent until he parked near a luxurious condominium high-rise sheltered by huge old trees. The look of the place gave her pause, and she stared at the dark building as Buck came around to her side of the car.

"You expected the cottage?" he said shortly.

"No." She hadn't expected anything; she hadn't thought that far ahead. But she had been hoping for a softer look in his eyes and a gentler touch than the possessive hold with which he claimed her arm.

She stepped inside the foyer as he extricated his key from the lock and flicked on a switch that turned on two soft lamplights. There was no easy-comfort cottage here. A stark-white carpet, very thick, led down two platform steps to a sunken conversational square; huge navy blue couches in velvet took up that space. Most of the lighting was recessed, and the accents were chrome; a white marble fireplace was flanked by bookshelves and a stereo unit. The bar was a Chinese lacquered affair with a navy shine, and there was a grouping of oils—none of them Van Gogh—but she could have drained her savings account and not been able to afford even one. The room was strictly masculine, elegant, austere, and very, very expensive. The look of the place was so very different from the comfortable assurance she always found in Buck that she felt suddenly, ridiculously frightened. There was a vulnerable flicker of silver in her eyes when she turned to him.

His jaw seemed to clench even more tightly. "Take off your coat. Do you want a drink first?"

The *first* grated. "I don't *need* a drink, if that's what you're asking," she said evenly.

"Fine. The bedroom's through there." He motioned and then turned away from her to hang up his coat. Since she'd neglected to take off hers, he did it for her.

"Was that supposed to be a calculated insult—or just an accidental one?" she inquired softly.

"Insult? But you've won, Loren. You can have it all just your way. No relationship or commitment. A body needs sexual release; that's nature. You haven't the time for commitments; you don't want to compromise; you've got your own principles that you won't give up for anyone. So an occasional quick roll in the hay is the perfect answer—"

She froze and turned away from him, closing her eyes for several seconds. A slap in the face would have been kinder. "You know I didn't mean what I said in the bar," she wrenched out. "I was angry. I was trying to make you angry . . ."

"But I think you *did* mean it. Maybe you wanted to see me, but on *your* terms, right? *Your* way, Loren, a stolen moment here and there. With no future. I could tell just by the way you looked at the condo that I'd done something unprintable by having money. Am I wrong?"

He wasn't wrong. He wasn't right either. He was just totally confusing her. No, in all honesty she hadn't approached him to talk about their future, but she certainly hadn't approached him just to go to bed with him. "Buck . . ."

"Am I wrong?" he repeated harshly. "Have you changed your mind about finding a place in your life for commitments, Loren?"

"I . . ." She swallowed without being able to speak. What she wanted and what she felt she could have were still two different things. "Listen . . ." But she had nothing to say.

Neither did he, yet his razor-sharp words were a shocking contrast to the evocative gentleness of his hands. His palm brushed back her hair, and she felt his lips, smooth and cool on the nape of her neck. His arms weaved around her waist, pressing her back against his chest as he kissed the side of her face and the hollow of her shoulder. She drew in her breath, confused all over again to feel what she did, a sweet rush of abandonment as if he'd never said a hurtful word.

His hands crossed, one cupping her breast through the black material, the other stroking her ribs, then down to her abdomen, then lower. She covered his hands tightly with her own, arching her neck back against him, a murmur at the back of her throat barely kept silent.

He found the zipper and the clasp at her neck. In a moment, there was a puddle of silk and chiffon on the floor. She was still wearing stockings and the silver sandals and her wispy undergarments, and she still hadn't faced him. She had a horrible feeling it was too late to face him.

This *wasn't* what she wanted, no commitments, no promises, no future. She could feel passion in her bloodstream, desire like a fever at his touch—his strength to her softness, the feel of his rougher skin against hers. But it was not the same. She wanted just what she'd had, the man who'd respected her enough to want to cherish and protect her for a lifetime. She wanted just what she'd thrown away.

"Too fast?" he murmured. "Isn't this what you wanted, Loren? Just free and clear and who cares?" He spun her

around; she was as trembly as she was tense, her eyelashes
spiking her cheeks in the soft lamplight.

"That isn't what you really think, Buck—"

"What *I* think, lady, is that it would only take one time
to teach you the difference between having sex and making
love." His mouth seared on hers as he scooped her up and
carried her into the darkness . . . but something happened on
the trip down that dark hall. His heart pounding against hers
gradually slowed; anger seemed to drain from him as he
held her close. Suddenly, his arms cradled; his lips turned
soothing and tender, erasing the aching pressure of his earlier kiss. "But it isn't going to work," he murmured. "I could
no more touch you that way than fly. Dammit, Loren, you're
not trembling because you're afraid of me?"

A year from now, she might smile; he sounded so shocked
at the idea. At the moment, she shook her head, meaning
it. Buck had a capacity to hurt her that frightened her all
the way to her soul, but it had nothing to do with fear that
he would physically harm her.

"People have a right to get angry," he whispered. "It's
part of caring, Loren. I could shout from the North Pole if
I thought it would make you see sense. But I wouldn't harm
you for my life. You must know that?"

"I know. Buck . . ." The bedroom was chilly and pitch
black; she was still shivering when he laid her on the soft,
furry spread, deserting her there. She heard the sound of
buttons being undone, his zipper. "We have to talk . . ."

"We've been talking. And we'll talk again. Later . . ."
The stockings were very gently, very firmly peeled off. His
palms slowly glided up her vulnerable flesh, from her toes
all the way up to her rusty curls, which he smoothed back
as he settled next to her, his voice as calm as melted butter.
"Loren, I need to hold you. Don't tell me no."

His leg shifted, and his arm swept around and molded
her close, his palms sweeping from her hips to her spine
and up until his fingers splayed in her hair. Soft lips teased
at her temples, her cheeks, her chin, and then suddenly

possessed her mouth with a pressure that was intoxicatingly provocative.

It was an effort to keep her hands firmly at her sides. "Buck, I did *not* come for this. I don't want you to think that. To see *you*, yes, but . . ."

He didn't seem interested in why she came, only that she was here. His mouth teased, his tongue flicking the smooth outlines of her teeth, the roof of her mouth, her tongue. Trust me, his mouth said as his tongue played a parody of love, thrusting into warm darkness, then withdrawing. Lazily, his palm arched her hips to his, reminding her of the much more powerful thrust and parry of love. She *had* loved him . . .

He didn't play fair. The same lazy hand took a leisurely sensual path around to the front of her thighs, skimming over the curling mound of hair, up over the abdomen and ribs she'd always hated; she was too thin. The palm closed on her breast as his mouth left hers. She was suddenly short of breath, her voice cracking.

"Buck, I can't *think* . . ."

"They're perfect, Loren," he said gravely. "Small but exquisitely perfect. Like all of you." His lips closed on her nipple, her breast swelled in his hand. His teeth grazed the taut peak, then apologized with a warm, soothing tongue, again and again. Her fingers made fists at her sides. She tried to shift, but then so did he, his mouth circling the other breast, his finger tracing the underside. He cradled her breasts, pushed them together, then licked the crevice he'd made. His touch was seduction, but so much more . . . There was tenderness, a worshiping of the feel of her skin, a knowledge of what moved her more than physical needs. He was loving her, trying to prove to her the value of what they could really have if only she would see it. And every inch he touched felt like gold, he had a Midas touch . . .

Her swelled breasts suddenly crushed to his chest. His mouth claimed hers yet again as he molded her to the length of him, his arousal pulsing between them. She couldn't seem to fight him anymore, couldn't even remember why she had been trying. There was a wild, sweet song that kept singing in her veins, her head, her heart . . . the song he was teaching her. She matched the pressure of his lips with her own, fiercely running her hands over him to make up for lost time. She felt as if she understood everything he had been trying to say, was hungry for him as she had never been hungry for anyone in her life, for his touch, for the look of him, for his mind and his laughter and his own special brand of loving.

His mouth clamped down on hers, meeting fire with fire. Gentle caresses turned fierce to match hers until she felt weak again; then his kisses softened, trailing down her throat to her navel, trailing down to the soft, intimate parting of her thighs.

"Buck . . ." she protested.

Toes curled, her throat arched back. A year later, he trailed back to her mouth and his fingertips traced the trembling shape of her lower lip. Her body was shuddering, long since acknowledging that she was still a novice at a game he had mastered ages ago, long since aware he had concepts of loving she'd never conceived of.

"You were married. Don't you know more than that?" he whispered teasingly.

She shook her head, tears of emotion glistening in her eyes.

His fingertips soothed back the damp hair at her temples. "We haven't even started, Loren. I could make love to you for the next ninety years, and there would still be more. This is only one arena; there are still so many more we haven't touched. Listen to me . . ."

She leaned over him, cupping her palm over his mouth. "We'll talk," she agreed. "Later."

Chapter

11

IT WAS THREE in the morning when she called home and was relieved beyond belief that Rayburn answered rather than Angela or Gramps. "I didn't want anyone to worry," Loren said hesitantly. "It's not exactly my habit to . . . that is, I don't think I'll be home before morning—"

"I understand," came Rayburn's quiet voice. "You went out for an early morning drive, miss, just before your grandfather came down for coffee."

She smiled wryly. "I don't think that'll wash, Rayburn, but I'd sure appreciate it if you'd give it a try."

She was up at dawn, a most unreasonable hour when she hadn't had more than an hour or two of sleep. Perching one one elbow, with a tender smile, she studied the insatiable man curled next to her. His legs were sprawled, and his hair all tousled, and thick, short black eyelashes brushed his cheeks. She'd better cherish such vulnerability, she decided, because he didn't show much of it when he was awake. In fact, there was no forgiving him at all for the way he'd behaved... the earlier part of last evening. Unfortunately, it was the small hours of the morning that lingered in her mind, memories of a loving touch that wouldn't stop even when they were both exhausted. Over and over, he'd drilled into her head and her heart and her body and her soul that they were a matched pair, that matched pairs were very rare, that only a fool would toss out the chance for that kind of love...

Now, with his arms curled around her and two comforters still tucked to their chins, she felt wrapped in a cocoon of love; as if she'd been a crazy fool ever to run from him. Yet her eyes flicked lazily over the bedroom she'd hardly noticed the night before... the costly satin sheets, the gilt and black original Japanese prints, a huge Oriental-style wardrobe, and just beyond a balcony view of lawn and woods and lilacs...

Buck made a sleepily protesting sound when she slipped out from under his arm, but he didn't awake. The room was freezing. She was definitely risking pneumonia simply by going to the bathroom so she detoured first to his closet, emerging a moment later with a thick terry-cloth bathrobe belted around her.

She didn't really fully waken until she'd splashed cold water on her face, borrowed his toothbrush and then his hairbrush. Only then did she really look at the bathroom, with its sunken navy porcelain tub large enough for two, brass fittings, and huge velour towels. The wall beyond the tub was a mirror, all of it. She looked at herself: the glow of color in her cheeks, the brightness in her eyes, the wild way her hair was sensually waving this morning, the silly non-fit of the bathrobe. Her toes were completely buried in thick, dark carpeting, and her lips were scarlet, like a permanent love bruise. She had been loved, long and well, and it showed. And she was in the middle of a room that was stamped with the mark of a very wealthy man, representing the kind of lifestyle she'd sworn she would never again be a part of...

She tiptoed from room to room, not wanting to wake

Buck, trying to refit her previous image of him with the
new one. She knew the Buck of jeans and walking boots,
the man who knew how to fix a hot-water heater. The man
who lived here had a closet full of tailored suits, and—she
flicked a finger on a table—a maid who kept even the
corners dust-free, a liquor cabinet and dining room prepared
for entertaining, and a study that was dauntingly filled from
floor to ceiling with technical books. If the place was es-
sentially masculine, it also reflected comfort and ease of
living, and there was a sensual feel to the decor and in the
kinds of paintings he had chosen. It was the home of a very
successful person who knew exactly what he wanted and
had gone out and gotten it. Like you, Loren? she thought
fleetingly.

She wandered to the kitchen and opened enough cupboards and drawers to have a feel for breakfast potential
and more immediately for coffee. As she added grounds to
the coffeemaker, she studied the little room and almost
unwillingly started smiling again. *Bachelor* echoed here. He
had been more than willing to sacrifice cupboard space in
favor of a dishwasher, microwave oven, coffeemaker, and
a myriad of other small appliances—the duties of his maid,
she guessed, didn't extend to cooking. The refrigerator confirmed that: a quart of milk was on one shelf, two dozen
eggs on another, fresh fruit on the third—and the bottom
shelf consisted of a lot of yawning space. The freezer was
bulging with steaks and exotic frozen dinners.

She found his newspaper, settled with a cup of coffee at
the kitchen table, and raised her feet to the opposite chair,
crossing her ankles. She was halfway through the feature
section when a second sense made her look up. Buck was
standing in the doorway, wearing a pair of jeans slung low
over lean hips and nothing else. His rusty hair had been
hastily brushed; there were circles under his eyes from his
night of no sleep, and his smile held more than a hint of
possessiveness that sent a feeling like warm honey directly
to the pit of her stomach.

"Good morning," he said groggily.

"Good morning," she echoed back.

"Someone seems to have taken my robe."

She cocked her head back as he came forward to drop a kiss on her mouth. "You can't be serious. You mean a thief actually came in and ignored all the luxurious goodies in favor of an old, beat-up terry-cloth—"

"Do *not* be comical first thing in the morning," he admonished, and kissed her again, his lips lingering on hers this time. He smelled of sleep and mint toothpaste and soap, the most erotic combination ever, she thought. Her hands instinctively splayed on the warm bare flesh of his shoulders, as his slipped inside the robe to stroke the sides of her neck. He half-smiled, drawing back from her, but there was a hint of watchfulness in his eyes. "Loren..."

Her smile faded slightly as she stood up. "I'll get you coffee and then breakfast."

"I can do that."

She shook her head and then opened the refrigerator to bring out a carton of eggs. She could feel his eyes on her back, searching, silent. In a moment, she had a bowl out and was whipping a dollop of cream cheese into the cracked eggs, then she poured the mixture into a heated frying pan and scrambled furiously.

"You were up awfully early for a lady who didn't get any sleep."

"I was spying on you," she said cheerfully, continuing to scramble the eggs as if her life depended on it. A cup of coffee was set in front of him, and a brisk kiss was placed on his forehead. "Something that wouldn't have been any fun at all if you were up and around and knew about it."

"And what did you discover?" he said wryly, but again he had a watchful look.

"Only the important things. That your maid's very good, but you don't allow her in your study. That you'll stoop to TV dinners, but only the fancier kind. That you don't miss a month of *Penthouse*, but *Field and Stream* has top priority in the magazine pile. That you're a formidable chemist, and that you've tried desperately to accumulate enough shirts so that you don't have to wash for a month." She scooped the finished eggs onto two china plates from the cupboard and then settled next to him at the table, bringing forks and knives with her.

"No one has the right to wake up with such perception," he grumbled, and scooped up a forkful of fluffy eggs. "Anything else of major importance?"

She finished her own eggs in record time before answering, but then she dished out approximately five eggs for him to one for herself. She picked up her coffee cup in both hands, looking squarely at him over the rim. "You're not kind, Buck," she said quietly. "You . . . *weren't* kind, earlier last night."

He waited.

"I love you," she admitted softly.

He sighed, finished his eggs, and reached for his coffee. "You wouldn't be here this morning if I hadn't played rough," he pointed out flatly.

"Not again, though. I won't be . . . taken over." Her voice was clear and definite.

"Are those the only ground rules we need to work out?" he questioned bluntly.

She nodded.

He leaned over, tenderly touching her cheek with his palm. "You may be pint-size, Loren, but you have as much steel in your makeup as I do. I don't want to take you over; I never did. I want you to stand next me. Haven't you figured that out yet?"

She relaxed for the first time since she had awakened that morning, but at the back of her mind was the fleeting thought that Buck was honest but did not necessarily know himself very well. He was used to taking over, and he had uncovered a weakness in her that no one else had. He would use it if she wasn't very careful. And she would lose him if he did.

The conference table took up most of the space in the small room off Frank's office. A few minutes earlier, it had been completely filled with the supervisory production staff. Loren had been asked to stay a few more minutes beyond the weekly production meeting, as had Tony, the finishing foreman, a very short, round-faced man with receding brown hair. Empty coffee cups still littered the tables, and the room was stuffy with cigarette smoke that had nowhere to go. Loren's eyes were riveted on her boss's face, but Frank was concentrated on Tony.

"We're going to have to lay off the entire department. I think you already guessed that from the sales report," he said gruffly to the brown-haired foreman.

Tony's face turned ashen. "Yes, sir. I understand."

"There's no choice. Not for now. We can extend the finishing work to the press operators and keep those jobs. Work may yet pick up by early summer, just as it always does when the automotive companies start their push for fall. But until then . . ." Frank averted his gaze from Tony's steady blue eyes. "There's no problem with your job, Tony. There'll still be finishing work that requires supervision; you've got your tool-and-die background, and quality control is more important than it's ever been. It may not be the work you're used to for a while, but your salary will stay the same."

Twenty minutes later, Loren walked out with Tony, past the carpeted offices to the production floor. "Come on. I'll buy you coffee," she said.

He shook his head, his eyes distracted. "It would just churn in my stomach—particularly machine coffee."

But he let her buy him the coffee, and not long afterward they were both in the square cubicle that was his office, overlooking the sixteen workers that made up his department. "Mark's just bought a car," he said absently. "Johnny's wife is going to have a baby."

She listened.

"John White—he's been footing his mother's medical bills. She's in the hospital."

She listened.

"Brad Howell—I should have kicked him out of here

four months ago. He's nothing but trouble, a complainer. But I swear that guy hasn't produced a single scrap part since he's been here. I've never had such a perfectionist." He poured it on. Layoffs were part of the economic climate; unemployment was on the front page of every newspaper. Statistics had nothing to do with working with a man every day, knowing his private life, arguing with and working with and caring about him. Loren knew them all, just as Tony did. And Tony, one of the least emotional men she had ever known—he never raised his voice, never showed temper—had tears in his eyes. "It's not that I don't understand there's no choice. And Frank, bastard that he is . . . he's kept the crew on three weeks longer than I thought he was going to." He shook his head, eyes raised to Loren. "How the hell is Johnny going to manage with that new baby?"

It was a full hour later before Loren made it back to her own office, and then she was in no mood for Janey's bright smile and determined flag down. "I've been paging and paging you—"

"I heard," she sighed, and half-smiled at her efficient secretary. "Unless there was a fire, there were simply more important priorities." Like easing Tony's grief. Grief, she thought absently, was exactly the word . . . and news of a layoff would spread like wildfire in the plant, produce an uneasiness and worry that came under her jurisdiction. She would have to find time this afternoon to be visible in the plant, to provide a measure of reassurance and the right words . . . and she wasn't sure she had them.

"The comptroller called. Something about Workmen's Comp. Peters from Wilding on some engineer who used to work here. That OSHA dude's coming for an inspection on Monday . . ." Janey grinned broadly, handing Loren the series of notes. "You'll have to wear flat shoes that day. Unless you've got a pair of high heels that come with steel toes. And last though not least . . ." Again a pert grin. "The boss just called. He wants to see you."

Loren frowned, raking her hands through her hair. "I just saw him less than an hour and a half ago."

Janey shrugged. "Oh, the whims of the powers-that-be . . ."

Loren smiled at Janey's irreverence. Her secretary was the height of propriety in front of those powers-that-be, but alone the two women had an unspoken alliance.

"So hold down the fort a little longer?" Loren requested.

"Catnip for a kitten."

Loren closeted herself in her office. On the back of the door was a small mirror—yet it was large enough to reflect rusty hair gone askew, a lack of lipstick, and a cream complexion that tended to pale when she was troubled. Snatching up her purse, she repaired impatiently, brush, lipstick, blusher . . . she hesitated at the perfume spray, seeing in the mirror's reflection a single daffodil on her desk.

It had been delivered anonymously that morning. So had the ones that had arrived every other day since the weekend. Buck was so damned smart, she thought fleetingly. A dozen roses would have raised her defenses, too expensive a thank you for services rendered. But a single daffodil . . . how was she supposed to fight such an offering?

She leaned over, smelling the fresh spring perfume of the perfect flower, feeling unaccountably renewed. She wasn't any less depressed or unhappy about the pending layoff; no amount of flowers could alter that. In a ridiculously feminine way, she just felt better able to cope.

A few minutes later, she stood in the doorway of the office of Frank's secretary. Rosemary was an attractive woman in her fifties and all but an institution in the plant; she reliably radiated Frank's moods like a barometer. "He's absolutely messed up the *entire* afternoon. I don't know who's with him, but he *wasn't* scheduled, and I know Frank wants these letters to go out . . . ." Rosemary's hands fluttered up from the typewriter keys. "Trade jobs?"

"But then, do you really want mine?" Loren asked wryly.

"Not on a bet!" Rosemary motioned with a courtly flair toward Frank's inner door. "Good luck. And, Loren—that mauve dress makes you look good enough to eat."

"Are you trying to warn me that Frank's in *that* kind of mood?"

Rosemary nodded, grinning. "And better you than me."

Yet a rap on Frank's door elicited an unexpectedly cheerful, "Come in." Anticipating Frank to be at his most moody and least manageable, Loren saw a beaming-faced boss who inconceivably showed the courtesy of rising from his chair to greet her. "As usual," he growled, "I page anyone else in the company but you, and they come running."

"I was up with Tony..."

"I expected that." A fleeting frown lined Frank's temples, reflecting Loren's own distressed feelings over the layoff; then the frown smoothed to an unexpectedly even smile. "Loren. Say hello to my impromptu visitor this afternoon—"

She glanced beyond Frank with a polite smile that immediately froze. For an instant, she could have sworn that jade-eyed giant was Buck. The next instant, she *did* swear it. His eyes were gleaming pure mischief, Buck-style, even if the dark brown business suit echoed a commanding assurance that would have put her totally on her toes if he'd been a stranger. He stood up, watching as Loren's eyes fluttered bewilderedly back to her boss and then to him again.

"Our business is done, Loren," Frank said pleasantly. "We owe Mr. Leeds a champagne dinner, which I rather gathered you might like to deliver..."

"What on *earth* are you doing here?" Loren hissed up to Buck as they walked the hall back toward her office.

"Talking shop."

"Shop? Your business is die cast, and Frank's is plastics. What possible...?" She moved to close the door to her office; it was a mistake. The moment privacy was even tentatively assured, she found herself half-spun around, facing up to him. "Are you crazy?" Yet his lips had no problem parting hers, at first coaxing boyishly for that moment of insanity, and then his mouth deepened, drinking as if he'd been thirsty all day. She went up on tiptoe, her fingers suddenly clenching in the fabric of his suit. His hands swept swiftly over the silky fabric of her mauve dress, down her spine, his fingers. splaying on her tiny taut buttocks. She could feel the hard brand of his arousal between them and forced herself to draw back, her cheeks flushed and her gray eyes brilliant.

"God in heaven, Buck. I'm at *work*—"

Janey buzzed, and Loren escaped to the other side of the desk, staring at Buck as she punched the intercom. "Just tell him he can do whatever he wants," she snapped to Janey distractedly and then rapidly closed her eyes on Buck's full-bodied chuckle. "No. Of course don't tell him that. I'll call him back . . ."

"Let's go," Buck said when she set down the phone.

"I can't."

"I've already cleared it with Frank."

But she regained some semblance of control on the other side of the desk. "It isn't all right with *me*. I have work I really have to do. I don't care what Frank says."

"So I gathered." His look said enough. In his company, he was boss in all arenas; no one talked back to him. She took in the way his brown suit fit his broad-shouldered frame and had to admit that if this were the boss who had paged her, she would have hit the decks running to answer his call. The glint in his eyes said he wasn't at all pleased at her *no*.

"I love the daffodils," she said softly.

A strange expression chased across his face. "I might just stop sending them if *you* don't stop returning the gesture. I hate to tell you what happened when the florist walked in in the middle of a staff meeting to deliver a single daffodil to my desk," he growled.

"Isn't a lady allowed a romantic gesture, too, these days?" she questioned whimsically. "You could always toss them out, Buck."

"They'll stay on my desk," he said gruffly. "Do you know, not a single woman has ever given me anything, Loren, beyond perhaps a customary Christmas present?"

She shook her head, smiling.

"I would like to think your gesture was romantic, and

not a mere making sure all the giving was exactly equal."
He sighed. "So I can't spirit you away this minute?"

She shook her head again. "And you still haven't told
me what you were doing in Frank's office."

"To hell with your boss. I came to see you."

"Buck."

He opened the door, and she went out with him toward
the lobby. "When Frank was talking research the other day,
it occurred to me that I occasionally cross paths with people
who might do business with him at the supply end—as in
the supplier of raw materials. As it happens, we do."

"I see. You just had so much free time floating around
that you just decided to drop by and develop a personal
relationship with Frank—"

"Personal? No. I have absolutely no interest in a *personal*
relationship with Frank. Actually, I've always preferred
women," he said blandly. "Particularly one about a hundred
pounds . . ."

She tried one more time. "So you just happened to know
about some plastics raw-material suppliers, even though
your business couldn't be less related—"

"Rarely, *very* rarely of course, I allow myself to talk to
people who aren't in die cast, yes."

Loren's skeptical probing died under Buck's heavy tones
of thorough boredom with a now-dead subject. She sighed,
pushing open the door to the front lobby to lead him to his
coat. His motivations always had been unpredictable, and
where they concerned Frank, it was difficult to keep up an
interested momentum. Much more interesting was the way
sunlight suddenly caught fire in his hair in the square
lobby . . . and the way he looked at her when he turned
around. Instinctively, she moved toward him and then caught
sight of the receptionist staring at her from the windowed
cubicle. She stepped back with a slightly flushed face.

Buck took her hand, drawing her out of the line of vision.
"Weren't you trying to remember to ask me to dinner Thursday night?"

"Yes," she agreed, laughing. Then she frowned, just a

little. "Buck, I'm rarely home by then—"

"Try." His knuckles brushed against her cheeks. "I have a friend. He's having an anniversary party that night. I want you to come; we can leave after dinner."

Her smile didn't alter, but the expression in her eyes did. Buck's wealth was enough of a hurdle, but that social whirl of elite society was another one she wasn't so willing to bridge. "I really don't have anything to wear for anything like that anymore—"

"Fine. Come naked." He brushed a swift kiss to her forehead and was gone.

"Going home?" Janey stopped in the doorway as she put on her raincoat. "It's past five, Loren."

"Can't manage it yet." Loren smiled from behind the mound of reports on her desk, pausing long enough to press weary fingers to the back of her neck. "In a little while, probably."

Less than five minutes later, Frank appeared in her doorway, his expression gruff and impatient. "There's nothing there that won't wait for tomorrow, Loren. I want you to leave regularly by five from now on, just like the rest of the peons. You're setting a bad example."

"Pardon?"

"As in—for me. How does it look if the boss leaves before his employees? Get up and out." He half-turned, tossing back at her, "If you've got too much work in this department, I don't know why the hell you haven't told me. Recession or no, we could easily have added a part-timer to the staff."

She opened her mouth and closed it. How many thousands of times had she requested help? She'd stopped asking when the worsening economic climate had hit the front pages of the papers, understanding what Frank simply couldn't do. "Frank, I can manage," she started uncertainly.

"Don't argue. Not this time," Frank said flatly. "I mean it, Loren. I want you out of here by five every night."

Bewildered, she stared after his retreating figure. Frank

was really the strangest man to work for. Brilliant in engineering, at a total loss when it came to situations requiring tact, stingy in some areas yet terribly warmhearted in others. She knew very well he was fond of her, just as she knew he had always taken advantage of her. But a simple, kindhearted gesture with no return expected was inconceivable from Frank. What on earth happened to him today? she wondered idly, and then rather quickly picked up her coat. There was that old saying about gift horses. And she was one tired lady who had put in a few too many twelve-hour days lately; her loyalty to her job and its people was intense, but if Frank was willing to lighten her workload, she was more than willing to go home and put her feet up.

Chapter

12

THE KITCHEN WAS alive with tantalizing smells and tastes when Buck walked in on Thursday. Loren dropped the wooden spoon in her hand, her eyes lighting to see him. "You're early!"

"Starvation. I could smell Rayburn's ragout all the way downtown." He winked at the aproned man behind her. Rayburn chuckled, turning to stir one of his bubbling concoctions at the stove. "You're running early, too, aren't you, Loren?" Buck continued. "I thought you rarely got home until past six."

"Hmmm. By some act of God, I seem to have extra help in the office," she remarked idly. "Anyway..."

Anyway, he looked delicious. Caramel pants complemented by a salmon and cream striped shirt and tan coat. The russet hair was tamed while the green eyes distinctly were not. He projected lazy strength and a potent virility, and she had the craziest image in her head ... as if she were a russet-furred fox being hunted by her mate, and she so clever, playing hide-and-seek, really praying he would catch her. "You look very handsome," she complimented him frankly. "I did just get home and haven't had a chance to change yet—"

"What is all this chitchat?" he demanded, descending on her. "I've missed you," he murmured as he gathered her into his arms for a kiss.

Her lips parted willingly. She closed her eyes to enjoy the firm, sensual texture of his kiss and the vibrant emotions he aroused so easily with his touch. The soft texture of his jacket folded beneath her fingers as she gripped it, thinking how unfair it was that every time he kissed her, there seemed less and less reason to think rationally, to do anything but throw caution to the winds.

A throat cleared behind them, and Buck lifted his head. "How are you, Rayburn?" Buck asked.

"Just fine, just fine." The throat cleared again. "Dinner will be ready in just a few more minutes."

"Hip doing better?"

"Much better." The men exchanged glances that Loren noted speculatively.

She took silverware from the drawer and passed back and forth between the dining room and kitchen, once Buck had gone in search of Bill Shephard to exchange amenities. Butter, water glasses, salt and pepper, but on the fifth trip back into the kitchen, the look that had passed between Buck and Rayburn still hugged her consciousness. "You never did tell me how you hurt your hip," she told Rayburn as she absently stuck fresh candles into the candelabrum.

"Oh, a car accident. About seven years ago," Rayburn answered, his soft eyes following her as she again paused by the stove for a last testing sip of the soup. He turned away, tossing a salad at the sink. "I don't know what I would have done without Mr. Leeds. His father was in the hospital at the same time. Gallbladder, if I remember right. He had a ton of visitors."

Loren's hands stilled. "So you knew Mr. Leeds before?" she inquired carefully. "I mean Buck, not his father."

"Oh, yes, Miss Loren. He used to say that there was no

point in visiting his father because he already had a roomful of people in there. So he'd take me up and down the corridors when I got to the point where I could walk . . ."

An hour and a half later, Loren was sitting on the bed in her room, strapping on white sandals with a hint of gold in the heels. She wore white crepe slacks with a blouson top, also white, with full shoulders, its tailored lines softened by the feminine, translucent fabric.

She added no jewelry, but for once was liberal with eye makeup. Her hair she brushed back severely and set in enameled combs to keep it off her face, then she stared at the results in the mirror. To begin with, the outfit was wrong. Her closet had an ample supply of working clothes and a variety of jeans, but nothing in the way of party wear beyond the slinky black dress she'd worn to Angela's dinner, and that wasn't appropriate either. To some extent, the stark white was almost dramatic enough to actually pass for a party, and it brought out her own dramatic coloring, coppery hair and pewter eyes. But she wasn't comfortable.

And she was not in a party mood. At least not in the mood for the kind of party she expected this one was going to be. She'd wasted a great deal of time when she was younger playing lounging games with the country-club set. It wasn't a world she wanted to get into again. And tonight her distrust of people with money was exceptionally high . . .

Buck was sitting in a chair in the library with his legs stretched out when she came downstairs. He put his book down promptly, standing to study her as she walked in. No smile touched his features, though his green eyes were sharply alert on her expressive eyes. "Lord, you're striking," he murmured. He would have said more, but she was bristling like a porcupine.

"Thank you," she said crisply.

His gaze followed her trim form as she got the coats, and she became conscious of the intriguing way the crepe fabric snugged over her bottom. She was a lady of textures for the evening. The soft white blouse contrasted with the rich, lustrous thickness of her hair. There was no metal-hardness of jewelry to mar the touchable quality that her looks invoked. And though she'd hoped the effect would be austere and cool, she saw in his amused eyes that she had totally failed.

"Are we talking?" he asked mildly as he held out her coat for her.

She glowered darkly at him. "You know damn well why I'm angry."

"I gathered some roof was going to fall in when you barely said a word over dinner in front of your family. It couldn't be that you decided Rayburn doesn't suit you?"

"I adore Rayburn. It's *you*. And the fact that Gramps and Angela went behind my back to go to you, as if I couldn't handle my own problems."

She waited, expectantly, for any excuse to hurl ninety pounds of temper at him. Buck opened the back door and ushered her through without saying another word, neither in apology nor explanation.

"I don't *need* him. If I had *needed* help, I'm more than capable of getting it completely on my own," she added furiously as he got into the car beside her.

Buck started the engine and backed out into the night. "Well, the thing to do then is just to let Rayburn go," he said mildly. "I had him helping me out for a while, Loren, but I just didn't have enough work to keep him busy. He's got some pride about honestly being needed so if *you* don't have enough for him to do . . ."

She averted her face, wondering vaguely what it would be like if she were a man his size and could meet him in some dark alley at midnight. "No one keeps me. That's the point. I can pay my own way, anywhere *I* want to go."

"I'm sure you can. Your pride alone keeps you in the upper income bracket, Loren."

He wasn't angry, but there was a hint of impatience in his voice, and she suddenly clammed up. She felt nervous inside, all muddled. In one arena, of course, she owed Buck, really owed him. Rayburn was a wonder. She loved the man, and he had fit into the family like one of themselves. And it was a wonderful, generous gesture, very much like Buck, to go out of his way to help.

So. Since the issue was settled and she had no intention of giving up Rayburn, obviously a measure of gratitude to Buck was in order. Unfortunately, her hackles were raised and her stomach was in knots. She didn't want gifts she couldn't repay in kind. She didn't want a relationship based on obligation. She couldn't stand owing anyone. And he was right about pride. She'd cut it all alone, and perhaps, she hadn't coped brilliantly. But she *had* coped, and she was proud of that, and for anyone to come in and solve her problems with *money*, something she simply wasn't able to do . . . Why couldn't she and Buck just live on an island? she thought fleetingly. Alone together the two of them could make it, she knew it . . .

It was not an island that Buck pulled up to a short time later. The house was an architect's dream, an expensive brick and stone affair built on a ravine. The house belonged to Buck's old school chum, Roger Long. A maid in black uniform opened the door for them, wearing an adorable and thoroughly pretentious little cap on her head. Loren smiled brittlely, already prepared for the house's interior by the look of the outside. She'd been there about a hundred years ago.

People were milling everywhere, the women dressed in everything from suede jeans to gold lamé. Sounds varied from the clink of glasses to the tinkle of jewelry to the kind of sexy laughter that had to be cultivated through practice at parties like these. No paired couples allowed, no sitting down, and there was a clear-cut pecking order based on status. There was also a kind of desperate enthusiasm to have a good time.

Loren glanced back at Buck to see an expression of grim distaste on his mouth. "Now you've got the excuse to vent your temper," he growled next to her. "Hell, I thought this was going to be a quiet little celebration. Not a circus."

"Personally, I love parties," she assured him pleasantly, accepting a glass of champagne from a passing man in a navy suit, who winked appreciatively at her. "Adore them," she repeated, glancing back at Buck.

His eyes were following the navy-suited bartender; they were shooting out buckshot. Green buckshot. "Loren, no one's going to miss us if we just get out of here."

She shook her head determinedly. "They're your friends. If you're worrying that I can't fend for myself in this kind of group, Buck, don't."

He glared at her. "Of *course* I wasn't—"

"Bucky!" shrieked a tall blonde in scarlet silk, who weaved through small clusters of people to throw her arms around him. The kiss was noisy and exuberant. "Wait until I tell Roger you're here. Oh, Buck, he's so mad at me— he *agreed* to this little party and then when I told him how many people were coming—"

Loren waved her fingers good-bye and slipped away, her smile bright as she wandered the crowded rooms. She had no intention of clinging to him. For that matter, she wanted it clearly understood that he was perfectly free to enjoy himself.

The decor of the house was chrome and pale gray, starkly modern and expensive, and faced onto a wooded ravine. All the sterility in, all the richness out; to Loren, it was the perfect symbol of what happened to people with too much money. The upstairs was more interesting. One jacuzzi. One steam room. Bedrooms. Mauve. Olive. Blue. Crimson— whoops, occupied. She took another sip of her champagne in the hall and found a second set of stairs that led down to the kitchen.

Four women were seated at the kitchen table, munching hors d'oeuvres, one without a front to her dress beyond two straps that hung down to her waist. There was a fifth empty chair, and Loren took it. Introductions were made, and it didn't take ten minutes before she blended with the group, bringing old skills out of cold storage to mix with these wealthy, bored suburban females whose chief exercise was honing tongues. Furs were the immediate topic of conversation.

"I doubt very much you'd be nearly as concerned with the 'endangered species' list, darling, if Howard had actually sprung for a coat for you last Christmas," a platinum blonde addressed a dark-haired woman.

The brunette flushed. "Howard can be *more* than generous, Marge..." She extended a long slender hand with dark red nail polish gleaming, the bauble on her finger designed to snare any stocking within a five-mile radius. The jewel was promptly judged, complimented, and examined, and then it was a case of around the horn. The platinum blonde flashed a ring of emeralds, and the bare-breasted wonder next to Loren sexily drew a long slim leg on the table to show off an ankle bracelet of tiny emeralds and rubies. "Christmas—red and green. But what on earth can I wear with it?" she wailed.

The others laughed and turned expectantly to Loren. She wore no jewelry, nor did she immediately have anything to say. "Whom did you say you were with, dear?" the brunette offered, dripping kindness.

"Actually, I didn't, but I came with Buck. Buck Leeds." Having admitted that, Loren thought wryly that she could hardly leave the group thinking Buck was less generous than Howie. "He forbid me to wear any jewelry tonight," she admitted conspiratorily. "You see, he'd just given me this lovely little three-carat ruby, and I lost it. It tangled up with this other chain I had—"

Buck's hands suddenly clenched on her shoulders like a vise.

"That's just terrible," said the vacant-eyed blonde, looking up at Buck with a speculative gleam.

"I'm still in disgrace," Loren whispered. Buck's pull on her shoulders threatened imminent traction if she didn't rise. She glanced up only long enough to catch three carats of emerald glitter in his eyes before she was herded into the other room. "So," he murmured as he all but pushed her through the crowded throng of people, "we're not exactly in a mood to behave ourselves this evening."

"Not exactly," she murmured back, retrieving a second glass of champagne from the same navy-suited waiter. This time she winked back. "Are you having a good time?"

"Watching you, I may yet. Unless you want to go?"

"Stay," she insisted pleasantly. She had to sip the champagne rather quickly to avoid spilling it when he grabbed her hand to pull her toward their host.

She relaxed for the first time that evening when Roger Long's notion of an introduction turned out to be a kiss on both cheeks and the sparkle of an approving gaze. He sported a curly Afro and mod clothes, but the smile was genuine—the first of that breed she'd seen all evening—and his brown eyes struck her as honestly warm. He was an attorney whose star was on the rise, abetted without question by the ambitious and willowy blonde who'd assaulted Buck at the door.

Unfortunately, Buck was drawn from her side into another conversation, and then two men walked up to Roger. Rather than hanging in uncomfortably as the lone lady with the three men, she quietly detached herself again. After finding a bathroom, she ran a brush through her hair and reapplied lipstick. Once she came back out, she found Buck still engrossed in conversation with another man and Roger. She wandered down a few steps to a second living room off the ravine.

In the far corner was an empty couch shrouded in semidarkness that offered a quasi-haven, at least for a few minutes. She curled up on the corner of the couch, slipped off one shoe so she could comfortably tug one leg under her, took a sip from her champagne, and just for a second closed her eyes. She should have known better than to come here tonight. She should have known better than to get involved in any way with a man with money.

"Are you new to the neighborhood? I don't remember seeing you before . . ."

Her eyes opened as she felt a depression in the cushion

next to her. The man with his hand on her shoulder was the All-American high-school football hero, aged fifteen years, prepared to be as lecherous on a couch in a crowded room as he'd undoubtedly been in the backseat of a car at a drive-in movie fifteen years ago. Loren gave a mental sigh of resignation. The conversation moved right along to the man's open marriage, as he established less than subtly that he was married, that he was looking, that he liked redheads, and that his wife didn't mind.

Loren beamed at him sympathetically. "Thank heaven we've broken out of the Victorian era," she agreed. "It's always been such a joke that a man or woman should be or even could be monogamous. The whole subject's a bore."

He loved her.

"The best thing about that kind of marriage is what happens to the children," Loren continued enthusiastically. "Naturally, the question of paternity arises. Do you have any children?" He opened his mouth in obvious denial, so she continued, "I can see the society of the future, where children are a completely communal responsibility..."

His hand edged back from her thigh in time for Buck to see the byplay. All-American was beginning to look restless. Buck, by contrast, was looking lazily relaxed as he folded his long length into a chair a few feet from them both, out of All-American's vision but clearly in Loren's. He sipped at the drink in his hand, simply watching with bland features, occasionally darting a look at some passer-by in the vicinity.

"There's a tribe in Ghana with marvelous sexual customs. The woman has the baby, and then she gives it to her mate's brother to raise. If she has another baby, that one goes to her mate's uncle. She never has to worry about raising her offspring herself; she can just go from man to man—"

"Yes," All-American said restlessly. "But we seem to be talking about nothing but children, darling—"

"We seem to be," Loren agreed pleasantly. "Don't you like children?"

"Of course. But—"

"They don't fit into your lifestyle?" Loren asked sympatheticaly. "Oh, well. Who needs children?"

Buck stood up. "Put him out of his misery, Loren," he said flatly.

The blond's head did a sixty-degree whirl, first around and then directly up, then flashing from Buck's face back to Loren, who was still smiling warmly at him. She patted his husky knee and leaned forward to whisper, "He doesn't actually share all of our views," before standing up.

Out in the cold silent night, Buck fastened the frogs of her raincoat and then let her lead the way to the car, encouraged by pats that connected unerringly with her bottom.

"I do not tolerate brutality," she told him formally when he finally had the heater going and they were headed home.

"You're kidding yourself. You invite it," Buck said bluntly.

He was *not* happy. She slipped off her shoes, leaned back in the seat, and closed her eyes. "Give it up then, Buck," she said softly. "That's not my world; it's yours."

"You're inviting it again," he responded dryly. "That isn't the kind of party I thought I was taking you to, and I told you that. At any rate, you wouldn't have given a soul in there a chance no matter what the guests had been like."

It stung more than a little that she knew he was right, that she'd arrived at the party with a preconceived stereotype of the guests and once there had made no real effort to seek out someone she might have been able to talk to. She'd given no one a chance, not even herself, but it had all started when Buck had interjected a financial aspect to their relationship by deviously insinuating Rayburn into the household . . . and her pride was still smarting. Stiffly, she sat next to him, her eyes still closed. Pride was very lonely company, and in trying to prove some obscure principle, she'd made a total fool of herself in front of a man she cared for far, far too much. It was a while before she cleared the lump in her throat. "Well, at least you could hardly have been irritated about one thing," she ventured.

"Meaning?"

"Didn't you like the way I handled Don Juan?"

"I enjoyed watching you. Is that what you wanted to hear?"

"Yes," she admitted.

"And the next man who puts a hand on your thigh with moonlight on his mind just might get his wish. Directly from outer space. Did you want to hear that, too?"

She smiled faintly. "Jealous?"

"And you weren't?"

When the scarlet-clad blonde had kissed him? When the bare-breasted beauty in the kitchen had arched her spine to show off for him? "No," she said honestly. "If you really like that kind of woman, Buck . . ." Then he could hardly like her. Not in any possible way that counted.

"Good," Buck said pleasantly. "Because I can count on both hands the number of women I've shared an occasional night with over the last few years. I'm glad that doesn't make you uncomfortable."

Her eyes blinked open, staring at the horrified stillness of a dark spring night speeding by, her heart knotting itself up in tight little bows.

In good time, he admitted, "Fib."

It was too late.

She believed it was a lie. It wasn't that, and it wasn't specifically those women. It was the jealousy that promptly clawed at her insides, an absolutely disgusting emotion when she knew rationally that at his age and with his potent sexuality there had to have been women. For that matter, the thought of one-night stands was infinitely preferable to what she suspected was the truth: that he'd had real women in his life, women he'd wanted to love, women probably more beautiful and experienced than she was and with far less troublesome problems. Women who'd probably jump at an offer of marriage, and for all she knew they were still ready and waiting in the wings.

"I hate you, Buck," she said impassively as he turned into her driveway.

Unsmiling, he turned the key and killed the engine. She closed her car door as he closed his, folding her arms under her chest for the chilly walk to the house. She felt a bleak confusion inside as he silently walked next to her, a frantic need to suddenly make things right between them again. She bent to fish the key from her purse and said in a low voice, "I don't hate you. And I haven't wasted a whole evening behaving like a kid having a temper tantrum since . . . I was a kid having a temper tantrum. But if you could try to understand—"

"I do understand," he said shortly. He unlocked the door for her and set both her purse and keys on the counter inside. "You're the one who doesn't, Loren. I want time with you. Not when you've got haunted circles under your eyes and are too tired to talk. Rayburn solves that. I involved myself for *my sake*, Loren, to get what *I* want, not because I was trying to *buy* you or place you under any obligation." He closed the door to the kitchen again, with both of them still standing outside on the porch. Only the soft porch light gleamed down on her russet hair and silvery eyes when he chucked up her chin to look at her. His lips were soft and cool, lingering. He folded her close to him, just hugging her to his warmth until, for some inexplicable reason, she simply felt better. Her fingers reached up to stroke his cheek, and he turned his head to kiss her wrist. Then he took both of her hands and held them down to her sides. "We have something, Loren. You know that, don't you?" he said quietly. "Even when I'm mad as hell at you, I'd rather be with you than with anyone else. You've got to let me show you that there's no reason to build up defensive walls—not with me."

She nodded and then simply stared at him as he strode out into the dark night. She loved that man. And he made it sound so easy . . .

She lay in bed that night and couldn't sleep. She knew both in her head and in her heart that there would never be another man like Buck—not for her. He monopolized all of her thoughts; she craved being with him; she needed his touch and his humor and his gentleness. She felt like spring inside when she made him laugh, when he responded to her touch, when she saw the tense, coiled businessman relax just being with her. She already knew she wanted a lifetime, that a few months or years would never be enough... So why was she still fighting him?

Yet it wasn't so simple. Depending on others had never come easily; too many people had let her down when it counted. Her parents, Gramps, Hal—when the chips were down, she was the one who had had to dig out from the rubble. She trusted herself, and it had been a long time since she'd unlocked any of those doors marked "Vulnerability." Buck's money didn't help. Money made for easy answers, those same answers that had destroyed her family.

He's nothing like that, she told herself. Loren, don't be a fool.

Chapter
13

LOREN BURROWED THROUGH her bottom drawer and finally emerged with the ounce of fabric that proved to be her three-year-old bikini. Slipping on the emerald bottoms, she then reached for the white cotton jeans on the bed, glancing out the window as she did so.

The Saturday morning promised a brisk spring day. The tulips had popped, and the flowering crab was one huge fuchsia ball; a hedge of white lilac sent up its perfume from just beyond the red maple. Trees and bushes were rustling in the stiff breeze, and the blend of colors and smells had her mesmerized for a moment . . . and then didn't.

She was hurriedly fastening the top to the emerald-green bikini when Angela popped into her bedroom doorway. "Buck wants to know if you're growing grass up here. What's taking you so long?"

"Hmmm." Loren grimaced, pulling a green and white striped cotton pullover over the bikini top. "We're going sailing on one of those little Hobie Cats . . ."

"So he said."

Loren put her hands on her hips. "Yes. Well, since it's not exactly swimming temperature, we're going to wear wet suits. Buck has his own, but he had to rent me one."

Angela had instinctively started grinning and collapsed on Loren's bed with a bounce. She settled in, arranging the pillow behind her. "So far, I still don't know why you're running fifteen minutes late."

"Because," Loren said flatly, "he took me off guard when he called last week. He wanted to know how tall I was. I told him five-three. He wanted to know how much I weighed. I told him one-hundred-fourteen. He asked me what size I wear, and I told him a nine."

Angela burst into chuckles.

"Listen," Loren said sternly, "that dress I bought on sale last spring *was* a nine—"

Her sister bent over, doubled with laughter. "So you made him rent a wet suit that won't fit? You could always wear high-heeled sneakers. If you could gobble up four of Rayburn's pies in the next five minutes, there's an outside chance you could gain a few more pounds—"

"Would you stop laughing?" Loren said wretchedly. "I'm twenty-eight years old and still feel like the runt of the litter. God in heaven. How could I have said anything so *stupid*..." She glared at her sister, but an unwilling smile appeared on her face as she listened to Angela's infectious laughter. "What *kills* me, really kills me, is that I'm a serious person. People respect me at work, can you imagine that? Intelligent human beings depend on me. Whatever got into me..."

"I think our perfect Loren has fallen," Angela teased. "You must have a terrible case, Sis. Someone once told me that only love brings out the mendacity in a woman's soul."

"Doesn't sound like Shakespeare," Loren said wryly. "More like advice from your friend Shiela." She burrowed in the closet for her sneakers, but not before she flashed her sister an affectionate glance. A few weeks ago, they had so rarely shared laughter... now everything was going well. Gramps had been sober a solid three weeks; work had let up; Frank was treating her like royalty; Angela was a ton less hostile. For the first time in years, Loren felt that the treadmill had finally slowed down. She was laughing more, had even gained two pounds...

She sat back on the bed to lace up the white sneakers, thinking fleetingly that money was her only worry. The van—the mechanic had told her she was throwing good money after bad after that last repair. The house *had* to be reroofed this summer, and whether Rayburn asked for it or not, she was handing him at least a token salary. "You haven't mentioned lately what kind of wedding you want," she said casually.

"A big splashy one with orange bloosoms and brides-maids," Angela said ecstatically. "Lots of people and danc-ing and champagne..." She looked at Loren suddenly. "I suppose I can't really have that sort of thing. It's expen-sive—"

"We'll manage absolutely anything you want," Loren assured her firmly. "But, sweetie, if you want that large an affair, we've only got two months to prepare for it." Men-tally, she was giving up the last of the good oils in the living room. For that matter, hand-painted china was all well and good, but sentimentality was expendable. The family silver had already been depleted, but there were a few more good pieces. It was just such a rotten market to sell anything...

"Loren, we may not get married exactly in June."

"Pardon?" Loren whirled from burying a bra and un-derpants in the bottom of her purse.

"I was talking to Buck," Angela said hesitantly. "David and I aren't any less sure, Loren, it isn't that. But like Buck said, it would be nice to start out with at least some new furniture, instead of scrounging for attic rejects. If I just worked one summer and could save my salary, we could get some furniture. I'd have time for Rayburn to teach me to cook something. I mean, I don't want to go into this like dead weight for David—"

Loren's jaw dropped.

"Like Buck says, exactly how long is ninety days, or a

couple of hundred for that matter? Would you believe we'll spend over four-hundred-thousand hours together if we stay married for life?"

"No," Loren said wryly.

"It's not that. We've got months ahead of living on beans. It just seems to me they'll taste better if we've at least got a new dining-room table to eat them on."

Loren listened, but she felt a crazy lurch of something in her stomach that she couldn't explain. The emotion should have been delight that *anyone* could make her sister see a modicum of sense. Somehow, though, she felt an unwilling sense of loss for all the dozens of times she had approached her sister with that same kind of reasoning and never gotten through.

"What did you do to my sister?" Loren demanded to Buck as he turned out of the driveway.

She was leaning back against her door, studying him. He looked completely different out of his business armor. A breeze ruffled up his hair from the open window. Sunlight glinted on his bare arms below a short-sleeved, white terry-cloth shirt; old jeans lay soft and snug on his thighs. His smile was lazy, seductively lazy, and she hadn't been able to look away from it from the moment they'd gotten into the car. "Your sister puts a lot of stock in the male viewpoint," he drawled, "unlike *her sister*. Who listens to no one."

She tsk-tsked teasingly. "You'd swallow up anyone who went in for that 'obey' stuff. On the other hand . . . I just might have in mind catering to your every whim today, Mr. Leeds."

"Do you?"

"I do."

"Come over here then."

Smiling, she pivoted around and stretched out, leaning her head back in the cradle of his thigh. His one hand left the wheel to stroke back her hair, and she closed her eyes. It was most evocative chemistry, the feel of his hard thigh beneath the nape of her neck, the feel of his fingertips on the silk-soft skin of her throat. The miles sped by; she felt wrapped up in a cocoon. She had him to herself for the entire day; she could anticipate the lovemaking that would happen sometime; she knew the whole day would be special. Happiness was such a simple thing; for the first time in her life she felt she could almost hold on to it, that it was something she could touch the way she could touch Buck . . .

"I want you, Loren," he whispered vibrantly from above her. "How long are you going to make me wait? *Why* are we waiting?"

That warm rush of sheer pleasure in her bloodstream stilled just a little. She stared up at him with soft silvery eyes. "I don't know," she answered quietly.

"I'm older than you are. I want children. Your children. I want to wake up with you next to me, and I *don't* want to have to make arrangements around two very busy people's schedules to make love to you. I want you *with* me, Loren." He took her hand in his, clenched it so tightly that it hurt, and she twisted up to a sitting position close to him, looking up at him with troubled eyes.

"I just want to be sure. Sure that I could fit into your world—"

He gave a sound of impatience, but the quick look he shot her was suddenly less tense. "You think too much. I'm going to get you so tired today that you just won't have the chance to think for a little while."

A short time later, they were both on the dock behind his cottage. The wet suits were lying on the dock; Buck was already stripping off his white shirt and jeans to put his on. The sailboat was bobbing next to them, looking to Loren as substantial as a scarlet toy in the breeze. Sunlight was whipping up a little froth of silver all over the diamond-shaped lake, and those same golden rays rested warmly on the golden skin of his shoulders, on his long, lean torso, the tight black swimming trunks, until he covered it all up with the black wet suit. He turned, as if just realizing Loren was still just standing and caught her eyes on him. He grinned, an unjust wealth of perception in his eyes. "My turn to watch you strip," he told her teasingly.

"I want to discuss that," she said firmly, hands suddenly on hips.

He started chuckling.

"No. I mean it. I want to discuss this theory. You put on a wet suit. The water comes between your skin and the suit, and your body warms up the water so you don't freeze to death. Right?"

He nodded and then came closer with a silvery glint in his green eyes. "I don't buy the theory," she said stubbornly.

"I'd tell you the number of people who've used these for decades, but I know better. There's only one way to convince you. Test it."

"That's what I want to discuss," she began, but those long fingers of his had already unsnapped her jeans, and to encourage them down, his palms slid intimately over her hips. She whirled around frantically to see if anyone was in sight.

"No one," he assured her. The top came off next, kisses laid like a series of buttons in a straight line. Forehead, lips, chin, the crevice between her breasts, navel. She was shivering, telling herself it was far too cold to be standing around in that spring breeze in a bikini. In a moment, she wasn't, as Buck helped her into the wet suit that was supposedly her size. He stood back, studying her with a little frown. She glanced down, bland-faced, at the legs that were just a little too long, the stomach a little too big.

"This *is* a small . . ." He shook his head. "Obviously, I should have gone into the children's section . . ."

"They probably just run big," she offered idly.

"Just tell me one thing. Did your parents make you drink coffee when you were a baby?"

She threw him a speaking glance, wasted as he had knelt down to reach the boat. A Hobie 14 Turbo, he'd labeled it; what she saw was a long, colorful sail still secured, beneath it a fiberglass deck of tiny proportions. Excitement quickened inside her as she studied the boat's sleek racing lines, yet she raised quizzical eyebrows to him, smiling. "You're sure there's room for me? I don't even see space for you."

"But then I work off the trampoline when we're sailing, sweets. You'll see. All you have to do is lie down and enjoy—and maybe shift your weight on occasion. But first, much as I hate to do this—"

She half-frowned curiously when he came toward her, then her eyes widened as he scooped her up in his arms and carted her to the end of the dock. As if apologizing, he kissed her swiftly on the mouth; then there was just a moment when she was swaying in the open breeze and had a few choice words for him. "Just *one minute,* Buck..."

The water swallowed her up. She came up sputtering, and totally, totally freezing. When she brushed back her sopping hair, she saw Buck next to her, treading water. "Now don't look at me that way. All you have to do is swim for a minute and you'll be warm."

The alternative was to stand still and turn into an icicle. He set a racing pace she could not conceivably keep up with, yet in trying, as much as she hated to admit it, she was warm in a very short time. The wet suit gave her a curious feeling of buoyance, and it was positively weird to feel a damp cool breeze on her face at the same time that her body felt almost bath-water warm. Finally, he motioned her back toward the bobbing boat.

"Ready to go sailing now?" he called back to her.

"Almost."

Water was such a marvelous medium. His two hundred pounds promptly lost their advantage. She dove underwater, aimed for his ankles, and tugged ruthlessly. She was treading water when his shocked green eyes surfaced a few moments later. "Ready now," she said cheerfully.

"Did you want to pay for that now or later?"

"At your convenience, of course," she quipped.

When Buck lifted her to one side of the boat, the whole craft lurched as if it would topple. When he got in the other side, it very nearly did. Loren lay still as he freed the long, tall sail and then positioned himself leaning out over the water, appearing to be supported by no more than a thin strip of vinyl cloth, the tiller in his hand. The boat responded to his every move like a lover anxious to please, maneuvering toward the center of the lake. "We'll go slow the first time around!" he called out to her.

The breeze caught his sail, and they went skimming the surface. Slow? she thought fleetingly. They were flying. Exhilaration and danger rushed through her veins; sparkly water sprayed up, soaking both of them. "Do you like it?" he called out to her.

"Love it!"

"Watch what happens in a turn, Loren." Horrified, she saw him shift his weight and was absolutely certain he was going under, yet the boat curled to match a jutting peninsula of land, and in a moment they were skimming fast and free again. Finally, they'd reached the end, and Buck motioned that they were ready to turn around and begin again. "Want to try it?"

"Is the Pope Catholic?" Carefully, she switched places with him, doing her best to imitate his movements as she felt the control of the boat in her hands. It was easy, until she tried a turn, shifting her body exactly as she thought he had . . . and the next thing she knew, she was in the water. Her head bobbed up in bewilderment, but before she could even blink, Buck's arms were hauling her up, and she could see the sailboat bobbing away from them.

His eyes were filled with concern. "You're sure you're all right?"

"Sure. What did I do so wrong so fast?"

He let out a relieved sigh and let go of her; she started to tread water, while he swam over to claim the boat. "We just discovered," he called back disgustedly, "that you can't take a great deal of credit in the way of ballast. As in that coffee your parents fed you as a child—"

"I was reliably fed milk. It's not my fault your parents bottled up joy juice for you—"

They were laughing as they got back on the boat. Over and over, they raced the length of the lake, each time faster.

Loren had the incredible feeling they were soaring at a thousand miles an hour, and she could not get enough of it. Part of that was just watching Buck. For her, the only challenge was in holding on, which on occasion was no small thing. But for him . . . she watched the satisfaction on his face when he'd conquered a speed that left her breathless or managed a tricky maneuver that left her heart dizzily in her throat. It was a sport of skill, not for the fainthearted. The rougher the obstacle, the better he liked it, and she loved that glimpse of the private man, of the challenge he had to take on, the joy he took in success.

"Had enough?" he asked her finally.

"No way!"

He flashed her a look of approval that made her heart sing. Another two hours passed before they finally secured the boat to the dock. Buck was breathing heavily, his wet suit half-unzipped from the sheer warmth of exertion, but the grin he shot Loren was expressive. "You've passed the last test. You may be spoon-sized, lady, but no one would ever call you a sissy."

"Thank you, sir." She vaulted up on the dock ahead of him, her bright eyes a denial that she'd just discovered every muscle in her body could ache simultaneously. She gathered up her clothes and then his.

"So. What are we going to do next weekend? Go hang-gliding or get married?"

Her hesitation was only momentary, but she could feel his eyes on her back. "Hang-gliding." She added lightly, "At least *next* weekend." And then added again, "As long as you've got the money for these crazy hobbies—"

His arm suddenly laced around her shoulder, drawing her up to him in a massive hug. "That's the first time you've joked about it. About money, Loren."

She looked up at him, pushing back the hair from her eyes, her smile suddenly wavering. "I'm trying, Buck." She took a breath and grinned scoldingly. "Listen, are you going to feed me or just stand around talking while I starve to death?"

Yet they didn't make it far. They stepped off the dock onto warm, dry sand and collapsed in mutual exhaustion. The rubbery wet suit was beginning to feel uncomfortably clammy and heavy on her bare skin; her muscles hurt; her stomach was grumbling; her hair felt like a wet mop. For a moment, it didn't matter. Buck pulled her up to cradle her against his shoulder, and they simply lay together, exhausted, totally spent, letting the spring breeze rush over them and the sunlight filter down on the warm sands.

Chapter

14

LOREN WAS IN Buck's bathroom at the cottage, staring at herself with dissatisfaction in the tiny circular mirror. The lake water had softened her hair to the point of total unmanageability; her nose was pink; and the white jeans and long-sleeved emerald top might show off her diminutive figure well enough, but the look was really not restaurant material. Buck was proving obstinate. And her purse had yielded only lipstick, perfume, and mascara.

"Listen," she said determinedly, as she came back out to find Buck pacing the small kitchen like a starving giant. "Maybe I haven't told you recently that I'm a fantastic cook. I could make you steak, filet mignon, frog legs, Chinese, Italian . . ."

Those hungry eyes suddenly fastened on her and then turned lazy, slowly taking in her huge gray eyes and the sun-kissed glow of her complexion, the way her russet hair lay thick and shining around her chin. He leaned back against the door, pulling her with him, snatching up her hands to hook them behind his head. "You did say I could have anything I wanted today, didn't you?"

"Which is why..." But she couldn't hold the thought. In sneakers, she felt tiny next to him, surrounded, outflanked. She could feel the warmth of his body through his clothes, and the sun had given his skin a burnished glow; He smelled just like fresh air and . . . Buck. His eyes caressed her until she felt dangerously disarmed; she felt like getting out a dozen white flags to celebrate surrender, and there hadn't even been a battle!

He stopped once to kiss her pink nose on the way down to her lips. "I do hate to take you out," he murmured. "There are times when I feel like closing you up where no other man can see you. You don't realize, Loren, how beautiful you are. Your hair feels like silk; your skin smells all fresh and soft . . ."

His mouth covered hers, his lips warm and smooth, tasting like the mint he'd just eaten. The kiss was a slow, gentle exchange that gradually altered to a more evocative caress. All those tense muscles from the day of exercise suddenly untensed for him, and she felt like sheer fluid inside, her body molding to fit around his harder contours, desire pulsing through her in a long, sweet rush. His hands skimmed from her hair to her shoulders and spine, and lingered, as they always seemed to linger, on the curve of her buttocks. Fleetingly, she thought that he favored that part of her anatomy. And fleetingly, she felt the richest sensation of being cherished, as she was surrounded by that web of strength and man.

The pressure of his mouth lightened, and then his lips left hers, but his eyes continued that conversation a moment longer, just as his hands came up to thread in her hair again as if he could not get enough of the touch of it. They were silent, just standing in the doorway, for hours. Years. He was like a Christmas present, all wrapped up and not opened yet. Fabric covered his shoulders, but she could anticipate the feel of his bare skin. He was standing, but she knew the weight of him covering her. And his eyes held promises of tenderness and passion, promises she knew he would keep.

"Ask me, Loren," he whispered vibrantly.

"Love me," she said simply.

"I do."

Her heart stilled for an instant. His hand brushed against her cheek again, and then he turned to lock the door; a moment later he was ushering her to the car. Silently, she sat on the seat beside him, knowing he'd wanted to make love to her, knowing she'd wanted him equally—and he hadn't. She stole a glance at him as he drove, having the strange feeling that he wanted something more from her this day, at this specific moment than a simple acknowledgment of love and desire.

The engine purred over the smooth roads to town. Silence rested easily between them; they were both tired physically, both rather somnolent as the sun settled down in the west, adding a pinkish glow to the concrete and cloverleafs of Detroit's inner city. He took her to Joe Muer's, a marvelous restaurant in one of the most dreadful areas of the city. Inside were spotless white tablecloths, tables crowded together, and uniformed waiters always in a rush. There was no season that the restaurant was uncrowded; the food was too good.

They were wedged in a table in the back; Buck ordered wine and food at the same time. They were both too hungry to wait. Loren was slightly uncomfortable with her casual clothes until the dinner arrived. Frog legs dipped in hot sweet butter weren't meant to be devoured in satin; cotton served very well. Buck had a blend of lobster and crab, and their eyes danced across the table. He gravely swiped a spot of butter from her chin; she watched his big hands trying to steal the last tidbit of lobster from its recalcitrant shell. Beneath the long tablecloth, her bare toes rested on his stockinged ones; they had both removed their shoes, which were well hidden under the table. If there were a hundred other people jammed into that restaurant, Loren saw none of them... Until they were served coffee and a dark brunette suddenly appeared at the table, dressed in cool blue silk.

"I thought I recognized you!" She laughed to Buck and bent down to give him a hug and a kiss. Bending back up, she glanced at Loren with bright brown eyes. "I'm Susan Harper—I... we knew each other a long time ago..."

"And this is Loren Shephard." Buck rose politely, but the brunette declined to sit.

"I just wanted to say hello. Really. And wish you well."

She left, and Buck's eyes bored into Loren's, his smile quiet.

She picked up her wineglass in an effort to pretend every muscle hadn't suddenly gone tense. She looked at the table, floor, silverware, and centerpiece before she finally met his eyes. "Was it serious?" she dredged up finally.

"For two years it was—but a very long time ago." He finished the last of his wine and looked at her. "She's a fine lady. And I wish her well."

They both stood up, ready to go. Loren's thoughts were filled with the brunette as they wended their way between the crowded tables. She loved Buck yet one notch more for the simple respect he'd conveyed toward the other woman. He'd started and finished the subject; she knew she'd never hear another detail. And she didn't want to know, but she suddenly felt the strangest restlessness. If the two of *them* ever ended their relationship, she'd like to believe Buck would still feel that kind of honest respect... but she knew she would never feel that friendliness, never be capable of the honest and easy greeting the brunette had offered to Buck so easily. There was nothing casual in her feelings for Buck. She felt too possessive, too private, too vulnerable... Did you even know you were in that far over your head? she asked herself wryly.

Night had fallen like a sudden silence in the streets. A light fog billowed around the streetlights as they waited for a parking attendant to bring Buck's car. From behind her, he turned up the collar of her jacket and pressed his lips to her ear. "Ask me," he said quietly.

She turned to face him. Moonlight splayed strange colors on his rough-hewn features, emphasizing a severity in line and bone out of keeping with the soft, dark eyes on hers. His words were an echo of the words in the cottage, and his look echoed that look.

"Tell me what you want, Buck," she said softly, troubled that she didn't understand. "I can't think of anything I wouldn't give you..."

"And you do, Loren," he whispered vibrantly. "You're so willing to give that I feel richer just being around you. All I want is to give that back..."

The car arrived. Downtown Detroit was lit up; the spires of the Penobscot Building and then the General Motors Building impressive landmarks in the heart of town. "Your plant's near here, isn't it?" she asked him suddenly. "Would you take me to see it?"

"There's nothing to see at night." But he made the appropriate turnoff. After a few minutes, he stopped the car at a watchman's station to be ushered through a gated fence, locked for the night. The main building was brick and two-storied; beyond was a huge asphalt lot and a warehouse that was three times the size of the office building. High-lows stood idle next to truck and trailer beds; barrels were stacked neatly... her own plant wasn't nearly as clean or well maintained. It was only a whim, her asking to see it, yet that whim took substance. She wanted to understand Buck, and she wanted to know every aspect of his life.

"That's all," he said shortly.

"Wait a minute," she protested as he drove around and headed toward the guard shack again. "I haven't seen anything."

"The offices are just offices, Loren. If you had some background in die cast, I'd be glad to show you around, but I'm afraid you'd just be bored."

"So bore me."

She saw it all. At first, Buck trailed behind her in the silent dark office building, half-amused at her intense curiosity and perhaps a little annoyed to be wasting too much of what little free time they had together. He answered her first round of questions in monosyllables, until they reached his tool and die department in the shop. The shell burst then, and for an hour she listened to an incomprehensible technical monologue that had no meaning whatsoever for her . . . yet she gained a new measure of the man.

He loved what he did. He loved pressure, and he loved the challenge of being the best in his field; he loved beating out a competitor, and he even loved the economy for putting obstacles in his way to challenge his ingenuity. His work force, the core of which had been with him since his uncle retired, was strong and stable. The only unstable element was his secretaries, and he admitted not particularly proudly that he seemed to go through two a year.

A pefectionist without patience, she labeled him silently. He *would* be impossible to work for. Janey had accused her of exactly those same qualities a dozen times . . .

"I didn't mean to get into all this," Buck apologized suddenly.

"I know that."

The drive to his house was strange. Loren had the curious feeling that some secret had been unfolding all day, yet she was finally too tired, too sated, to keep searching for it. Buck—she had learned so much of him this day. He had a thousand facets, very few of which she really knew, some of which it might just take a hundred years to know. Yet what she had learned of him had answered no questions. She knew only exactly what she had known before; that she craved being with him, that she felt caught in a spider's web of attraction she could not seem to free herself from, and that love kept growing helplessly, no matter what objections she came up with when they weren't together.

She stepped out of the car at his place. His arm folded around her shoulder, and she grinned up at him as they walked to the house. "You've totally worn me out," she complained.

"A little sore from all the exercise?"

"You're the one who did all the work on the boat."

"That's no answer," he chided as he fit the key in the lock.

"A little sore, then." She'd braced her legs for those hours on the boat; her thighs weren't used to that kind of punishment. And her arms ached a little for the same reason, but she had no real complaint.

Buck turned a switch as she absently walked down to the navy and white living room. Recessed lighting suddenly picked up the color scheme, and yet echoed the night's softness. She slipped off her shoes and collapsed on the navy velvet couch with an enthusiastic sigh, instantly cocooned in the luxurious depths of cushions.

"Would you like something to drink?"

She shook her head. "Not really. You go ahead."

He disappeared. She thought he was getting a drink. Instead, he returned a few minutes later with his shirt off, a quilted blanket in his hands, and a bottle on top of that. Her eyebrows raised in question.

"It's still cool enough for a small fire. Want one?"

The white marble hearth was fed cherry and beach logs, until there was enough of that flickering orange brightness for him to turn off the artificial lights. He spread the blanket close to the fire and then came to Loren on the couch, bending to kiss her—but it was not an impassioned kiss. More a communication of warmth, of . . . easiness between them. Gently, the green shirt was pulled over her head, the jeans tugged over her thighs. The bra was unsnapped. She looked at him. "Buck . . ."

One of his arms slid beneath her knees, the other behind her back. As he picked her up, she kissed his bare throat. His pulse there went frantic, yet he laid her down on the cover and skimmed off her panties, his hands almost impersonal. "On your stomach," he murmured.

She turned, facing away from the fire. On the opposite wall she could see his huge shadow kneeling over her, and she heard something, a popping sound. His shoulders in shadow took up that entire wall; she watched as he poured something into his hands.

Then she helplessly closed her eyes, feeling heated oil soothed into her skin under his palms. She heard a garbled sound of shocked pleasure emerge from her throat; she heard his answering chuckle. Suddenly, there were no sounds from either of them. His hands first slowly stroked out muscle aches and then kneaded in the slippery soothing heat of the oil. Her flesh felt like warm silk, and his hands were loving the fabric he had created, her shoulders, her back, her bottom, down over her thighs and calves; he missed nothing, even rubbing the oil into the balls of her feet, between her toes.

"Buck . . ."

Slowly, he turned her over, then reached for the bottle of warmed oil again. Silvery eyes met emerald ones. Her arms were lifted, massaged, laid back. He took a year to glide the oil over breasts, kneading warmth into one silken orb at a time. The fire crackled next to them, creating a very small world of light and shadow where no one else existed but the two of them. His face reflected intense concentration, his eyes still holding hers as the oil was soothed onto her stomach, then down to the most sensitive flesh. Her fingers curled at her side; her toes curled, and still she could not look away from his eyes.

His eyes were dark and grave, watching her. The sweet-scented oil and the touch of his hands had aroused the most sensitive and powerful sexual vibrations she had ever conceived of. She wanted him with a primal need; her desire was mindless and fierce and helpless. She read the same desire in his eyes. *Mine*, she read, *mine, Loren*. Fingertips knees, thighs, breasts . . .

She rose up on her knees taking the bottle of oil from him. Her flesh was golden, glistening and almost iridescent as she knelt over him, her small fingers stroking in the oil over his long legs. A thousand sensations seemed to rush through her bloodstream. She could see her shadow on the wall as she had seen his; she could see her breasts full and her nipples raised and the curve of her spine as she concentrated on giving him pleasure. She felt on fire, and she felt very soft; she felt the power of being a woman and the frailty. She took a breath suddenly and just looked at him.

Helplessly, she averted her eyes as she shifted her body, feeling a slight awkwardness when she wanted no awkwardness; she wanted the moment perfect for him. "Close your eyes," she whispered, but he wouldn't. He watched as she straddled his legs, as she very slowly took him inside of her, he watched her eyes close for those seconds and the way her hands trembled when she picked up the bottle of oil again. She hadn't touched his chest. She poured the oil between his male breasts, yet her hands were trembling; a little too much liquid dribbled from the bottle. Her palm glided the oil over his flesh, her body rising up to reach his shoulders, down again to cover his ribs. There was a faint smile on her lips, an acknowledgment of that rhythm, and her trembling ceased. It was her turn to watch him, to see the fire glow on his heated skin, to feel his hips shudder in tension beneath her, to watch his eyes change from a soft, sensual green to the glow of emerald on fire.

"Cap the bottle, Loren."

She shook her head. "I'm not done," she whispered. "I may never be done. Do you think you could die from wanting, Buck? Because that's how I feel."

She heard a long, low guttural sound in his throat. The bottle was taken from her hands, capped, tossed somewhere. He drew her down on top of him, and she felt for the first time the full length of his flesh against hers, the delicious slippery sheen of oil creating the most sensual heat between them. His lips seized hers, and long arms swept over her flesh. She felt like water flowing over him. She felt like Eve, her lustrous flesh offered like sin. She felt desire as she had never known desire, as if she could be consumed by it, as if there could be no end to the feel of his flesh on hers, as if she were caught up in magic, a dark, sweet, fierce magic... And she felt the force of him inside her, that filling up of empty space as if she'd been hollow without him, hollow and empty for those thousand years before she'd met him.

She murmured his name over and over. Every muscle suddenly tightened and then released in a long, low slide of unbelievable power. It happened again, yet still Buck strained for control, whispering loving words to her, encouraging her abandonment, his lips teasingly soft and then hungrily demanding, his hands tenderly caressing and then roughly possessive. She heard his low cry at the same time she felt yet another burst of ecstasy and then another.

A short time later, she was cradled next to him, his hands still stroking her back. Behind them the fire had died down to a huge bed of red-gold coals that radiated warmth and the softness of shadows. His fingers tilted up her chin, and he kissed her yet again.

"It's never been like that for me before, Loren," he murmured. "Can't you understand why I can't let you go?"

"It's you, Buck. You're the lover," she whispered. "Every time you make love to me..." She didn't know how to say it, but there was a sudden glistening of tears in her eyes.

The buzzing of the alarm was a revolting intrusion in the darkness. Loren's eyes blinked open, startled. She felt Buck shift next to her to turn off the maddening sound.

"What's wrong? What time is it?"

Buck's voice was groggy. "Four."

He shifted to sit on the side of the bed, shaking his head as if to force his body to awaken. Evidently it worked, for he turned back to her alert, aware, and half-smiling. "You've had two hours sleep, lady. Time to get on the move."

"You're crazy," she said.

"Up."

From the fireside, they had moved to the shower, and from the shower to the big sunken tub and still another round of lovemaking. It was past two before they slept. Loren watched with disbelieving eyes as Buck pulled on jeans and a sweatshirt, then reached over to swat her bottom sharply.

"*Up*. We've only got a few hours left. And we're in a hurry."

"We are?" she repeated vaguely.

"We are."

She pulled on the jeans and green top she was frankly sick of and stood patiently while Buck brought the brush over and made a masculine effort at restoring order to her hair. She started laughing when they brushed their teeth together in the bathroom. "You wouldn't like to fill me in—?"

"No. Not particularly."

"I had a feeling that was going to be too much to expect."

Yawning, she trailed after him to the car. It was still black outside, the quietest time of the night. Single streetlights beaconed on dew-drenched grass; spring flowers released their most potent perfume in these predawn hours. She snuggled next to him in the car, and he drove down past the oldest part of Detroit, past Grand Circus Park, past the city's new Renaissance Center. Only a few cars ventured in either direction; even the Motor City was tired at four in the morning. When he parked, she still had no idea what he had in mind, but she was fully awake by now, curious beyond toleration and totally enchanted with the mystical outing.

She understood, a few minutes later. "We're actually going to walk it?" she said incredulously. "I didn't even know you could."

The Ambassador Bridge stretched the miles between the United States and Canada, a tall, graceful structure over the Detroit River. Huge freighters rested in the water below as they started to walk across, Buck's arm firmly around her, her cheek still half-snuggled to his chest. A single car passed next to them, and then there was no one. She had the strange illusion that the bridge was theirs, that they owned the city because they claimed it as theirs for that short crazy time.

He didn't stop until they'd reached the center of the

bridge, and then he turned her around, drew her back against his chest, and threaded his arms around her waist. She could feel her breath almost stop as she looked back to the city's skyline. The fresh, crisp scent of that early, early morning blended with the look of moonlight diamonds on water, and the skyscrapers were all lit up. The night lights reflected on the water, mirroring back a second fairy-tale metropolis of gentle motion and color.

Slowly, that changed. Slowly, black turned to charcoal, then to rose. The sun came up from the east, casting a rosy glow like a magical blanket on a Sunday morning city still sleeping. Buck suddenly turned her to him, entwining his fingers in her hair as he kissed her roughly, hungrily. "Ask me," he said vibrantly. "Now, Loren."

She finally knew what he wanted. She couldn't have said why. Perhaps it was the sudden rough pressure of his mouth, as if he could force her into submission. More than that it was the tender love in his eyes, for something he wanted to share with her. A hint of all the things he wanted to share with her.

"Dammit. You haven't played fair from the moment I met you," she whispered up to him.

His lips claimed hers again. "Ask me."

"All right then. Marry me, Buck!" Her tone was helpless, almost angry. She just couldn't seem to fight him any longer. In some part of her mind, she knew there were rational things, important things, that hadn't been settled, not for her. But in another part of her mind, there was that magic of his, the magic she felt whenever she was with him, a magic she knew she couldn't live without . . .

Chapter
15

SUNDAY EVENINGS HAD always been hectic for Loren. Hair, clothes, nails, facial, leg shaving, and last a long, scented bath: all her female puttering had always been crowded into those last hours before another work week began.

This Sunday, though, she had barely stepped into the bath before she was stepping out of it, wrapping herself in a white terry-cloth robe and padding barefoot down the hall to knock on Gramps's bedroom door. He glanced up from his book when she came in. He loved to read spy novels, and his look was a little impatient.

"I only want a minute, Gramps," she assured him, and then shoved her hands into the deep pockets of the robe and took a breath. "You didn't say anything downstairs about Buck. Angela and Rayburn were vocal enough, but..."

Gramps marked the spot in his book with his finger and just looked at her. "He's a fine man, Loren. I never thought you'd have the sense to pick a man like him. I thought you'd find a good-looking boy you could regularly push around, and knowing you, I thought he'd be dirt-poor." There was a spark of teasing in Bill Shephard's voice, yet she knew he was serious. "Buck certainly doesn't have to fear that he's getting a gold digger, now does he?" he added ironically. "Angela often talks of the short time she remembers when the family fortunes were still flying high. You haven't a single good memory from those times, do you, Loren?"

She hesitated. "I remember the house filled with people. Dad's laughter, and that special perfume Mother wore . . ."

Gramps put the book aside. "You were too sensitive as a child," he said thoughtfully. "Somehow you always had the idea that your parents would love you more, give you more of themselves, if they weren't so frantically caught up in their social world. I used to watch you, being hurt. Time and again. I used to watch you, and I used to think that you had to toughen up, Loren, because no one could survive life who was that vulnerable."

"Gramps . . ." Loren swept an absent hand through her hair. She'd come in with a clear plan for discussion, which seemed suddenly confused. "I grew up a long time ago. None of that matters anymore."

"I hope it doesn't. I've been worrying that it still does. The way you put us first, Angela and myself, over anything to do with your own life, as if your intention was to right things from a long time ago. It's long past time you learned the art of selfishness, too, Loren. Have you ever read Ayn Rand?"

She smiled suddenly. "A long time ago." She perched on the edge of his bed, shaking her head scoldingly at him. "We're digressing. I want to talk to you about Buck. I want to know how you feel, what you'd like to do, Gramps. If Angela and I both marry—"

William Shephard groped up from the bedroom chair and stood up, walking to the window. He looked like a very frail old man with gentle blue eyes. "That's what I mean. *Stop* thinking of us, Loren. I'll cope, or perhaps I should say Rayburn and I will cope together. You're really asking about my Fridays, and the answer is—I don't know." He sighed. "I'm an old man, and in many ways I feel my life was really over a long time ago. You're the one who counts now—"

"That's just not true," Loren said swiftly, her expression brimming with compassion.

"It is. And forgive me for saying this, but it isn't Angela's grandchildren I want to see, it's yours." His soft blue eyes focused directly on hers. "That man adores you, Loren. It's over, the stress. You'll have financial security, children, laughter. You'll be protected, and you'll be spoiled. You've never been spoiled." He sat down and picked up his book again. "He's perfect for you. Apart from which, I don't approve of your going out and not showing up again until the middle of the next morning," he finished gruffly.

"Now, Gramps," she chided his bent head wryly, "you just told me what a good quality selfishness is. And I have to say I couldn't care less what anyone thought of what time I came in in the morning."

Her grandfather glared impatiently at her. "That's one of the reasons I know he's perfect for you. Now get out of here, granddaughter. James Bond just got into Russia..."

Perfect for you.

Loren shoved the van into drive and set out on that rainy Monday for work. The first day of May was sheer cats and dogs. Rain slushed on the windshield, and the wipers were already working full speed.

She hadn't slept well, for no particular reason. She had told all of them about Buck, and the consensus was unanimous: Buck was perfect for her. Total approval. And her family's feelings mattered to her... though not, perhaps as much as she'd always thought they did. She was so in love with Buck that she couldn't think straight. During the hours apart from him, she suffered something like withdrawal pains. He was passionate, generous, bull-headed, a little arrogant, whipcord smart, sensitive, domineering, and he had a sense of humor. Some of that made her furious. All of it she loved.

She braked for a red light and opened a window. The

defroster was having a tough time competing with the rainy fog on the windshield. Involuntarily, she shivered a little. It wasn't that cold, but it was damp. Her raincoat covered only a lightweight short-sleeved jersey dress. She felt a little like crying and couldn't have said why. All she had to do was think of Buck and their time in the boat and their lovemaking and the look in his eyes on the bridge, and she could not regret her yes.

The light changed, and she pushed gradually on the accelerator. Bad driver or no, she crawled in weather like this. Maybe it was just the rain affecting her mood, she thought fleetingly. Maybe it was that before she met him so many people needed her. Her life had been one long race to survive the onslaught of burdens, and she had built up a crazy kind of pride in her ability to cope. It had been so hard for her, and Buck had only to wave his little finger... There was Rayburn for Gramps. Angela's rebellious impulsiveness was tempered the moment Buck talked to her. Suddenly, she had the help in the house she'd so badly needed.

She had no way to match his gifts. She had only herself to give him. Almost fretfully she tried to understand her own brooding mood, so unlike her. It was just... everything she'd worked so hard for suddenly seemed inconsequential, as if all her efforts were for nothing, as if she wasn't the capable, reasonably successful lady she'd thought she was... but a failure. For not being able to help the people she loved on her own, for not even being able to help herself. All Buck had had to do was walk in...

Oh, stop it, she told herself wearily. Just stop thinking. For one thing, you were firefighting all the time; you never had the chance to get above the conflagration of troubles to just breathe. And for another, you're ungrateful, and that's disgustingly *petty*. And for yet another, you know better than to try to think when you haven't slept well. Your head is mush. It's just not the time.

Having avoided the slippery expressways because of the rain, she turned off on still another side road, now only minutes from work. The rolling residential street was narrow and lined with soaking oaks and maples. It was like driving through a tunnel in the downpour. She slowed still further, noting the speedometer at twenty-five when a car honked in exasperation behind her. The speed limit was thirty-five. "Sorry, buster," she muttered. "Just be grateful you're not behind me in a snowstorm. I get out and walk the van in that kind of weather."

She rounded the crest of a hill, noting a little bright yellow car coming in from a side street. She was almost at the bottom of the valley when the little VW, instead of braking at the stop sign, accelerated through it. Frantically, Loren wrenched at the steering wheel, knowing with an instantaneous sense of horror that she was going to hit the car. Skidding tires shrieked in her ears, and she heard the crunch of metal on metal even as the crash shuddered through her body; her forehead jolted forward to collide with something hard on that tender skin, then snapped back.

It was over in seconds. For a short time afterward, Loren was paralyzed in total shock. With violently trembling hands and her heart in her throat, she wrenched open the door, climbed out of the van and with stricken eyes saw the battered, crumpled-in side of the VW. A woman's head was leaned back against the driver's seat, eyes closed, and Loren could hear the faint sound of a baby crying.

"Oh, my God..." Her own emotions were buried. She stumbled over to the little car, pounded frantically on the window, and then tried to open the bashed-in door. It wouldn't give, but the woman inside... her eyes fluttered open, her face all white, her expression dazed.

"I saw the whole thing! Are you all right?" Through rain-soaked lashes, Loren glanced back to see a man in a navy-blue sweater approaching her from one of the nearby houses. There was no time to answer; she was already whipping around to the other side of the car to open the passenger door. In a second she could see the baby was still strapped into its protective car seat, screaming its head off. The mother, a youngish blonde, could not have been whiter if she'd painted on a ghost mask; her fingers were moving in slow motion up to her mouth.

Loren reached in to grasp her hand. "Are you hurt? The baby seems fine, but she's..."

"I... she's all right. That's what I... Julie was crying. And I was trying to hurry home. She's wet, and she always cries when she wets her diaper. I..."

For just an instant, Loren felt like screaming, just as the baby was. If the woman had just *looked*, even if she hadn't stopped for the stop sign; if she'd just been going a few miles an hour slower...

"The baby was crying," the mother repeated hysterically. "I was just trying to get her home. Ted will kill me. I..."

Loren's fingers tightened protectively on the woman's wrist and then she let her go, her voice low and soothing and totally in control. "Everything will be fine. Your baby is unharmed. You look more shaken than hurt..." Loren glanced back out through the pelting rain, saw the flashing lights of a police car approach, and a group of neighbors milling out of their houses obviously willing to brave the rain to see what was going on. Over the strident screams of the baby, the man in the navy sweater came forward again.

"Miss, you really shouldn't be talking to her, you know. When it comes to an insurance settlement—"

"Oh, for godsake," Loren said disgustedly. Again she glanced around. There were three women, all rather grand-motherly in shape and dress. "Could we get the baby out of the damp?" she requested in general to all of them. A gray-haired woman in a dark dress stepped forward as Loren leaned back into the car. "Would you like me to take the baby?" she asked gently.

The bewildered mother nodded. She was rubbing her forehead in a dazed reaction. Loren handed out the diaper bag and then reached in again to unhook the straps of the baby's car carrier. In a moment she had the burden of blankets and furiously crying child in her arms, and she cuddled the baby instinctively for a few seconds before handing her to the gray-haired lady. "I'll take her, miss. I'm the house right there. You've no need to worry. I raised five of my own; she'll be fine—"

The baby was snuggled to an ample breast and sheltered from the rain. Loren turned back to the child's mother. "Come on now," she said calmly. "Let's see if you're hurt . . ." She lifted the baby's car carrier to the back, out of the way, and reached in to help the young mother out of the car. The blonde moved awkwardly over the gear shift, raised her legs out, stood up shakily with Loren's help, and promptly burst into tears.

It was a nightmare. The little VW was totalled; it took more than twenty minutes in the back of the police car for the two policemen to get a coherent story out of the mother to corroborate Loren's. Finally, the man named Ted arrived to take his wife and baby home, and Loren allowed the enormity of what had happened to sink in at last. She had nearly killed two people. It didn't do any good to know that it would not have been her fault or that there was nothing she could have done. She nearly killed a young woman. A baby. A *baby*.

When she finally stepped out of the police car, she saw the wrecked yellow VW being attached to a tow truck. The look of the smashed-in side made her hands shake violently. The garage owner approached her. "I'm afraid your van's not driveable either, miss. I'm not saying it can't be fixed, but there's no chance you'll be driving it for a while."

She had forgotten her own vehicle. In comparison with the VW the van fared a thousand times better, of course; it was the bigger, sturdier vehicle. But the front still looked like an accordion . . . "What do you want me to do?" the man asked patiently. "It'll have to be towed off the street, miss."

So it was towed off the street. Loren was offered the use of a telephone by the grandmotherly lady, and she called Janey at work. Janey arrived less than fifteen minutes later, took one look at her boss's face, and said, "Why don't you just let me take you home? I can hold down the fort for a day."

Loren shook her head. There was the regular staff meeting on Mondays; she had a dozen other things that had to be done today. She'd never fallen apart in a crisis in her life, and she was not about to start now.

"I told Frank," Janey admitted. "To begin with, he was looking for you first thing this morning . . ."

"Go home," Frank told her bluntly, the moment she walked into the staff meeting.

But she didn't go home. In fact, she made every effort to shine in the meeting. Her facts were clear and concise, her presentation clear, her smiles brilliant. The accident was over; all she had to do was put it out of her mind. No one had been hurt. She whipped through her work that morning in triple time and wasn't alone in her office again until noon.

She had to call the garage. The repairs on her van would cost more than her insurance coverage, and the young couple were evidently as underinsured as she was. Loren put down the phone, leaned back in her chair, and lifted her ninth cup of coffee that morning to her lips, trying to ward off the sudden, stupid, unreasonable welling of tears. After all, she'd known for a long time that the van was going. It was just a delayed reaction to hearing that baby's frantic cries for those few instants before she knew the child wasn't hurt.

She put the coffee down, leaned forward, and pressed her palms to her temples. There was a raised spot on her forehead, hidden by a wave of russet hair. Irritably, she moved her fingers over so that she could at least press out the tension in the rest of her temples.

There was a sharp rap on her half-opened door, and she glanced up. A tall, intimidating frame suddenly filled the doorway. She had never seen Buck's eyes loaded with such desperate tension before. She swallowed and blinked rapidly, perhaps not quite fast enough to totally erase the glaze of moisture in her eyes.

"Why the hell didn't you call me, Loren?"

She shook her head and put her hand out to stop him from coming any closer. If he touched her, she knew darn well she was going to be folded in that strength of shoulder and tears would follow. "Just . . . don't."

"Don't be silly, Loren—" He came a few steps closer, and she shook her head more wildly.

"It matters to *me*, Buck. I *hate* women who fall apart. Just don't touch me for a minute. Please!"

His whole face seemed to tighten for an instant, and there was a flare of something stark and lonely in his eyes. Then he turned, and his eyes fixed on her raincoat hanging from the back of the door

"No," she said simply.

"You look as though you used bleach for makeup today." His voice was so normal, that Loren thought she'd imagined the anguished look in his eyes.

"Thanks," she said, with a monumental effort to sound normal herself.

"I'm starving. I shrivel up to five-foot-one if not fed lunch on time." He lifted the raincoat, a stubborn glint in his eyes. Arguing would have as much effect as trying to scale a brick wall barefoot. She sighed. "Think of the fat little brandy I'm going to order for you," he coaxed. "Think of the beating I'll give you if you don't come. Think of—"

"All right," Loren said with exasperation. She put on the coat and then turned back to him, trying to smile. "But I'm only coming for the beating. If I drink anything at lunch, I'll float all afternoon."

"Coming up, one beating, after we let them know you're leaving," he said gravely. But as she made to move past him, his hands suddenly laced across her shoulders. Her startled protest didn't stop his determined inspection of her arms to test for bruises. In a remarkably small number of seconds, he'd discovered the swelling blotch on her forehead. "Head hurt?"

"No." She had the horrible feeling he might just have stripped her to the buff to check for injuries if she hadn't

pulled away and darted into the hall. "Buck, I'm *all right,*" she hissed furiously up at him.

Yet it was the first time she'd felt steady all morning, when he tugged her close to his side walking out to the parking lot. He smelled fresh and warm and familiar, and the feel of him was like coming home. But those feelings warred with others. It was all . . . off-balance again. She was needy once again—needing him. It never seemed to work the other way around. She knew she was still shaken up, that there wasn't a rational thought in her head, but she resented needing him. Terribly.

The restaurant was quiet and dark and nearly empty. The "fat little brandy" rested beside Loren, sipped once. Buck, for all his claim to hunger, had ordered coffee for himself. In front of her was a clear consommé and a double order of plain, ordinary toast, all of which she was pushing around in haphazard fashion. "I don't understand how you knew," she said absently. "Did Janey call you?"

"Frank called. Which he should have done several hours before," Buck said gruffly, taking another sip of coffee. He hadn't taken his eyes off her from the time they entered the restaurant. "I didn't ferret out a thirty-thousand-dollar savings for him in raw materials from the goodness of my heart. I've got empathy for any man in the top chair, and a fool could tell he was a genius in the engineering line, but he lets his purchasing agent sit around on a constant coffee-break."

"John is rather that way," Loren admitted vaguely and then suddenly raised startled eyes to him.

"What's wrong?"

She just looked at him, feeling a helpless welling of confusion inside. Anger, hurt, and that something shaky that had haunted her all morning even before the accident. "How could you?" she demanded.

"How could I what?" He looked bewildered.

"*Interfere,* Buck. You're the reason Frank gave me the

part-time assistant, aren't you? You're the reason that I'm suddenly no longer taking home reams of work. That day you were in the office..."

Buck's eyes shifted to the coffee cup. "Don't be ridiculous, Loren. I never told him to hire an extra person in your office. I never *told* him to do anything."

She set down her cup, glaring speechlessly at him. No, he'd never *told* Frank anything. It wouldn't have happened that way. He just did Frank a major and very expensive favor and dropped her name and the connection. And Frank had suddenly scrambled to treat her like a favorite niece.

Buck was glaring back at her, his features just as strained as her own. Quite obviously, he'd never really intended to tell her; it had just slipped out. "It's not the time to discuss it," he said shortly. "Another time, Loren, you can set up the boxing ring. Right now you're going home."

"I am *not* going home. I am going car shopping."

He took a look at her pale complexion, at the dark gray eyes glowing like coals, at the determined set to her jaw that, in spite of its minute size, was really remarkably like his own. He sighed and leaned back to finish the last of his coffee. "There are times," he said mildly, "when the Detroit Lions could probably hire you as a fullback, as is. They'd probably even manage to win a few games in the season."

She didn't smile. "I *have* to have transportation."

His own smile faded. They stood up, and he nudged at the small of her back to urge her toward his car. "What you *have to have* is some emotional letdown." His tone was a deep-throated growl. "You're as strung out as a whip, just waiting to lash back." He closed the door with a little clip in her ear. When he got in his side, there was controlled patience in his voice. "Just let me take you home, Loren. You can use the New Yorker until you really feel up to looking for another car. I can handle—"

"*No,*" Loren interrupted furiously. He was right in everything he said. She was an emotional mess; she couldn't even hold a coherent thought in her head; she belonged home, and there was no horror of a hurry over some ridiculous car. She wanted to obey, to let him take charge. But irrationally all she could think of was that she was turning into a doormat. "Look. I don't expect you to waste a whole afternoon. I'm more than capable of shopping for a car on my own. It's not your problem—"

The look he shot her was deadly. She knew immediately that she had stepped over a forbidden line and had a startling vision of Buck virulent in anger. Worse, she glimpsed the fleeting bleakness in his eyes again and knew she'd hurt him, terribly.

"It's not *my* problem?" he echoed. "You're not *my* concern, Loren, particularly when something's happened to you?"

"Buck, I didn't mean that the way it sounded."

"I think you did." He stabbed the key in the ignition, and the engine roared to life.

Chapter

16

THEY DROVE IN SILENCE. Loren's head ached from the swelling bruise on her forehead. She felt exhausted and strung out and confused.

She glanced at Buck as he drove, at his craggy features, the deep-set green eyes, the jutting jaw, and the sensual mouth now firmly compressed. His suit was Italian; she'd just noticed. The economy of line emphasized his broad shoulders, and he was a powerfully forbidding man when his jaw was set just so.

She longed to reach out and touch him. Desperately, she craved the protective embrace he had offered her so often, and just as desperately she wanted to erase her rashly spoken words. She hadn't meant to shut him out by implying her life was none of his business, and she hated herself for hurting him.

Yet she didn't touch him. He had hurt her as well. He had no right to interfere in her workplace, and the blow to her pride was sharp and unbearable. It wasn't just that . . . it was everything. Frank, Angela, Gramps; he'd stepped in and taken over. All of his actions were done for her; she knew that. It was just that in his view, she must seem like a puppet, as he capably moved the strings that affected her life. It wasn't how she wanted him to see her. A very capable, confident, bright, even rather successful young woman—that was how she wanted him to see her because it was what she was . . . at least until she'd met him.

Buck turned into a car dealership, and Loren tried to refocus on the more immediate problem at hand. She frowned; a Cadillac-Oldsmobile dealer wasn't anywhere near what she had in mind. "Buck," she said quietly. "I can't afford this. There's no point in my even looking here."

His green eyes pinned hers. "We're going to leave money out of this one," he warned her. "I'm not suggesting the top-of-the-line gas guzzler or an engine with more power than you can handle. I *am* suggesting transportation that doesn't crumple at the first minor bump in a parking lot. Now are you really going to argue with that?"

She felt she was on a downhill toboggan run and couldn't get off. She got out of his car, looked around, and had only to read the first sticker prices to know there wasn't a car in the lot in her price range. She knew Buck had every intention of buying the car for her, just as she understood that the taut nerves were not all on her own side. She'd seen the way he looked at her when he first arrived in the office and knew knew he'd suffered a frantic drive to her plant when he'd discovered she'd been in an accident, but she could not seem to grapple with anything beyond a head that kept pounding with increasing anxiety. And she simply could not let him pay for the car.

"I really think I would like to look at something smaller," she said finally.

Buck drove her where she wanted to go in complete silence. A bright rainbow of compact cars were all lined up, bug-sized, and Loren walked a little ahead of him in the drizzle, with a salesman trailing after Buck. She peered into several cars, finally finding one that had almost no chrome up front and none of the gadgets that brought up the sticker price.

"Would you like to try it out?" the young salesman asked hopefully.

"Yes." She glanced back at Buck for the first time in the last fifteen minutes. Her effort to smile died. His face was granite. Turning back to the salesman with a stubborn look, she repeated, "Yes. I would like to drive it, if you wouldn't mind."

Yet when she slid behind the steering wheel, the pounding in her head tripled; she felt suddenly cold all over, and her hands turned clammy. This was exactly what she wanted, exactly what she could afford, and the car was really an attractive little runabout. But then so was the little lemon VW the mother had been driving that morning . . . the one that had crushed like paper even in a slow-speed accident. She had a sudden vision of herself zigzagging around semi-trucks on the expressway in this little red car, and somehow her palms were so damp she couldn't make the ignition key turn. In fact, suddenly she couldn't seem to move at all.

The driver's door opened abruptly. Buck didn't even look at Loren's suddenly white face. His arms reached in, and though for a moment her legs argued with the steering wheel, her face was buried in Buck's chest a moment later. He just held her, rocking her back and forth in the middle of that crazy parking lot until the shuddering stopped.

"Is there anything wrong?" the salesman asked uncertainly. But his voice was muffled; one of Buck's hands was at the back of her head, stroking her hair, over and over.

"Nothing," Buck said pleasantly. "We just decided we were only in the market for Mack trucks today. Thanks for your time."

"I . . . pardon?"

"You can take the keys out of it," Buck said flatly. As in take a hike, mister.

The footsteps clapped on pavement and then faded. Buck sighed and pressed his hands very gently on either side of

Loren's face to lift her eyes to his. His mouth rubbed fleetingly on hers, as if touching base. She felt a rush of comfort.

"I keep living it over and over in my head," Loren whispered wrenchingly. "I'm not a good driver. A thousand times I've been too distracted. But not this morning, Buck. *This* time there was just nothing I could have done, and she . . . had a baby. The baby kept crying, and I kept thinking that I could have killed that baby . . ."

He folded her close again. Her eyes were filled with stinging tears, and desperately she swallowed and reswallowed the lump in her throat. He didn't seem to care, but she did. She was not going to come apart at the seams in the middle of a car dealership. She touched aching fingers to her temples, drawing away from him. "Dammit. I *have* to have a car," she said distractedly. "I can't just keep thinking about it. I *have* to be at work tomorrow—"

"And you will be." Buck steered her gently back to his New Yorker. "I'll take care of it, Loren, I promise you. But for right now, I'm taking you home."

She rocked against the car seat as though it were a cradle, closing her eyes as Buck drove. Those few minutes when he had held her were over. Her head was pounding again, the same disturbing refrains. It had happened again; he had taken charge, and somehow she was doing things his way. And it was wrong. Everything was all wrong. Old ghosts haunted her, and she couldn't seem to dismiss them.

He stopped the car in front of her house, and she looked outside. Sunshine was glistening on rain-drenched grass, the trees were whispering in the warm, drying breeze. Flowers were blooming, and the birds were going mad with spring fever. All she could feel was despair. She turned to Buck with agony in her eyes. "Buck, I don't want you to take care of the car."

He sighed with exasperation. "Loren, we've been through that. I refuse to discuss money with you when you're upset."

"You don't see, Buck." Tears suddenly glistened in her eyes. "You never will. It's just not going to work." His expression went stark and cold, as if he suddenly understood she was not talking about cars, but about the two of them. He opened his mouth to talk, and she shook her head wildly. "I feel . . . drowned. Before I met you, I felt reasonably good about myself, can you believe that? Then you came into my life, solving problems in short order that I'd been trying to work through for years. Angela and Gramps. A thousand things I thought were monumental. I met you, and in a few hours I was crying all over you. I actually went chasing after you in that bar. I behaved like an absolute fool at that party. And then you give and give and give, Buck. What do I have to give you back? I feel like less than what I was, as though I have less to offer. Suddenly, I'm nothing and have nothing to give. I can't handle it! I don't want it!"

He drew back as if she had hit him, pain echoing in his rugged features. "Loren," he said quietly, "I can't believe you really feel that way. Listen to me—"

But she wrenched at the car door to get out. "I *do* really feel that way. I wish I didn't. I tried a long time ago to tell you. About owning people, about being bought. That love changes color when it's all cluttered up with obligations and mismatched give-and-take."

"Loren—"

"I'm sorry. God, I'm sorry." She would have stumbled out if his hands hadn't clutched at her, jerking her around to face him. For a moment, they just stared at each other, Loren with tear-filled, desperately determined eyes. Through that blur, it seemed that Buck's face was magnified, and he was very, very still. In his eyes, she could read shock and anguish and love and anger but also a sudden cold finality, as if he finally understood that she had meant what she said.

"I've battled through those brick walls of yours before, Loren. If I haven't gotten through to you by now, I never will," he snapped curtly with a flatness that frightened her. "If that's how you see my actions, as buying you . . . if dammit, that's really how you feel when you're around me—"

"It is."

He let her go. She watched him put his car in gear and

drive out. She stood there, swallowed a thousand tears. and turned away when he was completely out of sight, completely out of her life. She walked into the house, fielded shocked questions from Gramps and Rayburn about the accident, mounted the stairs to her room, and collapsed on the bed. She felt weak, ill, drained. She was afraid of crying for fear her grandfather or Rayburn would hear her. She had to concentrate so hard to keep from sobbing that at last sleep stole on her, and she fell into an exhausted, restless, empty oblivion.

Loren opened sleep-scratchy eyes to ribbons of sunlight slanting on the bed. Sitting up, she glanced at the clock, and thought dizzily that it was impossible to sleep for better than sixteen hours and wake up still feeling totally exhausted. *What have you done?*

She forced herself up, took one disastrous look in the mirror and headed for the shower. A few minutes later, she was dressed in a lilac linen suit, very crisp and fresh, that cinched in her waist to Scarlett O'Hara standards. Makeup masked her pallor, and a brush restored life and vibrance to her hair. She studied the mirror again. There was really nothing she could do to alter the agonized look in her eyes.

Downstairs, Gramps, Rayburn, and Angela were all at the kitchen table. Usually, she was already at work before the group gathered for morning conversations. They greeted her smiling, and Angela impatiently motioned her to the window while the others exchanged silent glances. All she could think of was that at least her makeup had worked; no one was looking at her as if she resembled a mummy. She reached in the cupboard for a cup. She badly needed some coffee.

"Aren't you going to look?" Angela demanded excitedly.

"Look at what?" She turned back with a puzzled frown and finally glanced out the window at Angela's insistence.

The car was a silvery mauve, shining in the morning sunlight. The upholstery appeared to be a pearly gray, and chrome glinted like mirrors. The color was feminine, and the look was plush, without being oversized. Loren stared, as still as a statue.

"*Say* something," Angela said exuberantly. "God in heaven, it's not every morning you wake up to find a fairy godmother's been there in the middle of the night. The keys are in it. Whoever your guardian angel is, Loren, I'd like to have a little discussion with her—"

"Loren?" Gramps had been studying her; his voice was suddenly laced with concern. "What's wrong?"

"Nothing." She drew a ragged breath, picked up the phone, and dialed work. Janey was predictably frantic; Loren had never been late for work before. The secretary was considerably taken aback to discover Loren was taking the day off. Her boss hadn't even taken her vacation days in the last two years, had only missed four days in four years because of illness. When Loren hung up the phone, the family were all staring at her. "Would it be so terrible if I just took off for the day?" she asked brightly, with a little defensiveness.

"You don't mean you're actually going to play hookey?" Angela teased.

"Loren, what is *wrong?*" Gramps demanded, getting out of his chair.

"Nothing." She smiled, radiating cheerfulness. "I would just like to be by myself for a few hours. Does anyone mind?"

Gramps sucked in his breath. "No, of course not. But—"

"Fine." Her purse was on the counter. It was so easy. She just walked out the door, down the steps, got into the horrible, horrible car, and started the engine. It purred. She had never had an engine that purred. Of course she didn't now; it would have to go back to him. He was crazy. He had promised he would take care of her transportation, but of course that was before the argument. He wasn't liable for that promise. A very long time ago, she had stopped believing in promises anyone made her; they were never kept. What was he trying to do?

Obviously, she had to get the car back to him. But not

now. Soon. In an hour. Just this minute the car was her only means of privacy, and she was desperate for privacy. The first miles slipped away while she tried to convince herself that she wasn't terrified of driving after yesterday, and also that she hated Buck for putting the damned thing in her driveway.

Quiet roads led to more quiet roads. In an hour, she found herself on the tree-lined streets of Ann Arbor. The sidewalks were full of jeaned coeds. Carting armloads of books, the boys next to them looked just as terribly young, just as serious . . . Loren got out of the car and walked. At some point, she stopped to find something to eat, and then she walked again; later in the afternoon she stopped at a motel. She couldn't bring herself to go home, and for some unforgivable reason she was putting mileage on that car that wasn't hers. The motel manager looked at her as if she were a bit crazy; she didn't discover why until she'd locked herself in the motel room. Tears had made a mess of her mascara; her makeup was blotched; the linen suit looked like accordion pleats.

What have you done? She slipped off her shoes, folded down the blue bedspread, and leaned back against the rock-hard mattress, staring at a print on the wall that looked remarkably like a Rorschach ink blot in blue and gold. She saw Buck's face in it and looked away. She bunched her hands into fists and rubbed them hard into her eyes, like a child angrily forcing back tears.

She got up and turned on the television, and a few minutes later just as restlessly turned it off again. For an hour, she soaked in the tub, then got out and put on her wrinkled suit again. She sat back on the bed, determined to think it out. She tried not to think of Buck but just herself. About how important it had always been for her to succeed, to do well, to cope no matter what life threw at her. To be independent, to be self-sufficient. To not need anyone. She'd always envisioned any man in her life, any love, as added to the periphery of her life but not really denting the core. She never wanted anyone in that deep, not into her real

needs as a woman. Not where she was vulnerable...
Women these days were incredibly strong and proud of it,
and she had led the pack.

She got up again and tried the television a second time.
It was already past the news hour. Sit-coms were thriving.
She turned it off again, opened and closed drawers, found
the Gideon Bible chained to a desk, wondered why anyone
would ever steal a Bible, wondered how many years it had
been since she had been in a motel room. Thousands. With
Hal, on one of their thousands of pleasure trips. Meaningless
pleasure trips. She tried to summon up a picture of Hal in
her mind, but all she could see was Buck.

They were not the same. She'd tried very hard to convince herself that Buck was like Hal, like her father, like
Gramps, even like Frank. Buck just refused to fit the mold.
He kept his promises. He *had* maneuvered her, but never
for his own gain. To use her, to take advantage—she knew
it wasn't so. And he spent his money on comforts, but those
comforts didn't rule him.

She had loved those different men in very different ways;
they had all hurt her. So she had built up mountains of
protective defenses... she understood it all suddenly, very
clearly. When it was too late, she thought fleetingly. She
needed Buck like she needed breath, and suddenly she
couldn't breathe.

She stood up again, put on her shoes, ran a brush through
her hair, and walked outside. It was dark out, a warm, tangy
spring night, the stars like a web of metallic fabric in the
sky. There was no one in the deserted motel parking lot;
the only car was her own. She got in, locked the car doors,
and turned on the inside lights. For the first time all day,
she stared at all the little circular dials. The chrome glittered
back at her, softly shining.

Putting the car in reverse, she drove out of the parking
lot, leaving the windows down. The brisk breeze cooled her
cheeks as she drove aimlessly for hours. Midnight passed.
One o'clock, then two. It was close to three when she found
herself on a rutted road that was spring-muddy, surrounded

by trees and silence. At the end of it was a diamond-shaped lake, and just in front of that was a little cottage where every window reflected a lonely yellow light. The New Yorker was there. She couldn't have said in a thousand years why she hadn't gone to the condominium first. That was where he should have been; it was the middle of a work week.

She parked the mauve car behind Buck's and stepped out, trembling almost violently, her face pale. Her hands were shaking so much it seemed better just to leave her purse in the car; then for long ridiculous moments, she tried to decide exactly why it mattered where on earth she left her purse at all. Obviously, it made no difference.

Before she had taken the first step toward the door, it opened. With the light behind him, Buck's face was in shadow, but she had heard the way the door wrenched open, and she could see steely tension in the way he stood there a cold statue, his eyes like dark lights boring in her direction.

Her heart sank that inch below rock-bottom.

Chapter

17

LOREN STOOD STARING at his still form in the distance. She read no welcome in his silence, but then she hadn't really expected one. She didn't really know what she *had* expected. It didn't matter; she'd had to come, and for the first time in two days her head seemed clear, no longer churning with anxiety.

Unconsciously, she took a single step forward and then stopped, her palms just slightly extended and her gray eyes huge with pleading. "Don't turn me away, Buck. Please. I don't expect you to forgive what I said yesterday, but you have to listen." He didn't move, and tears suddenly welled in her eyes. She tried to smile. "I was jealous of you, Buck. Can you believe it? You could cope so easily where I couldn't, and I've been living on pride for so long that it felt as if the rug had been pulled out from under me. I was frightened, and I felt vulnerable, and just being with you brought out needs in me . . . needs I didn't want to believe I had. Needs I suddenly couldn't ignore. You touched every nerve . . ."

Still he didn't move, and her legs suddenly seemed shaky.

His eyes were on hers, she could see that in the darkness. His breadth of shoulder was like a memory of comfort no longer offered. "I think I might have worked through that," she continued. "But what I couldn't seem to work through was feeling that I had nothing to give you, Buck, not in return for what you'd given me. I don't mean money. I mean the real gifts you kept heaping on me, a listening ear and support and sharing and humor, the way you make love . . ."

The giant statue moved, a swift stalk in the darkness that closed in on her, snatching her out of that lonely silence and crushing her in strong arms. "How could you be so stupid, Loren?" he growled passionately. *"Nothing* to give me? How could you be so blind that you couldn't see how much I needed you? I've had every policeman in this state out looking for you; I've got a man at the condominium; I've got Rayburn up all night by the phone. You ever disappear in my life again and I swear I'll—"

His hand clutched in her hair, and his mouth crushed down on hers like a searing brand. She felt the most delicious, hurtful pressure . . . He broke away, staring down at her. In the moonlight, she could suddenly see his face, his eyes fired with love, his brows creased in anger, his jaw furiously set. Her heart surged with joy, with laughter and lightness and relief.

"I was wrong, Loren. To interfere. Especially in your job. You were so damned strong and so damned set in your ways and so damned sure of yourself that I didn't know how else to infiltrate the fortress. I never meant to take anything away from you. I never meant for you to feel that you hadn't done well managing your life. That's exactly what I love about you. The way you do cope, that cool head of yours, that sensitivity to other people, and those smiles no matter what life's handed you. Your laughter even on the darkest days . . . I need that, Loren. I need you.

"There is no other woman I ever felt would stand up to me, stand next to me, no one else I ever felt such an intense feeling of sharing with. You offered love, Loren, before you knew about the titles and trappings; do you have any idea how precious a gift that was? And we argued, Loren. That was part of it—finding a woman I could live with through good moods and bad. You fit like my other half. And you say *you* felt vulnerable? I felt torn in two when you said I made you feel like *less*. All I ever wanted was to make you feel like the beautiful, loving lady you are. The idea that I in any way made you feel cut down, diminished... I went home and cried... why the hell are *you* crying?"

"You are," she whispered. There *was* a certain crystal in his eyes. His arms wrapped around her like a haven, and his lips found hers again in that spring night. She answered kiss with kiss, touch with touch, promise with promise. She felt cloaked in love, surrounded by the whole velvet fabric of emotions finally set free. She understood his needs as she hadn't before; it mattered. She understood, too, that she had freely offered love but not trust, that trust was a very expensive commodity in her life, and that he had just bought it, lock, stock, and barrel. She had so much to tell him, and she wanted to tell it all to him with touch. Each caress seemed to invite another until suddenly Buck reluctantly pulled back with a husky breath.

"Loren," he growled. "I still have to call the police."

Her fingers still lingered on his sleeve, the slightest of frowns creasing her brow. "Why on earth did you ever call them, Buck? I phoned work; I told the family I was going out. There was no need for anyone to worry—"

"I was *worried* at ten this morning. It is now three-ten. A.M." He pushed her ahead of him toward the cottage, patting an affectionate, half-scolding commentary on her bottom. "The police may not honor a missing-persons call in that short a time. They honored a search for the car—come back here!"

She'd darted ahead of him but now half-turned. His hand latched onto hers. "Stay in touch," she was ordered gruffly.

She stayed in touch while he phoned the police and then his condominium; she called the family herself. Her eyebrows lifted wryly when that was done. "Why don't we just put it in *The New York Times* that I'm staying the night here?"

"Do you really want to waste time making *another* phone call?"

She shook her head, laughing, and then sobered. "No," she said softly. "I don't want to waste any more time, Buck." Her eyes met his, and she thought . . . riches. The richness of need and the richness of wanting and the richness of love.

Loren climbed the stairs to the loft ahead of him. There was no light upstairs, but a bright silver moon shone through the open loft windows. From there, Loren could see the still, silent lake, could smell all the spring freshness that suddenly had meaning again. She looked for a minute and then turned back to Buck. He was standing at the loft opening, still, watching her, and her eyes suddenly turned soft, her smile grave. "Buck. It really won't be easy."

"No." He moved forward until his fingers could reach the blue linen buttons of her suit coat. Slowly, he undid them, one by one, and just as slowly slipped her jacket off. "I want to protect you, Loren. To spoil you. And I'm going to. And you're going to fight that."

Her fingers were busy with his tie; it was half-off anyway. When that was on the floor, she worked the smaller buttons of his shirt. Her fingers splayed on the warm, smooth golden muscles of his chest. "You're used to being boss, Buck, but so am I. We're going to argue." She smiled fleetingly up at him. "You never did understand about the car. I can't just take it like that . . ."

He turned her around. The silky pink blouse beneath the suitcoat had tiny buttons in back, at least a dozen of them. She watched the lake and felt his hands trembling, and she loved him so much that moment she felt like crying. Like laughing.

"We can be married in three days. *Then* we'll argue about the car." The blouse was pulled from her skirt and slipped forward to the floor. He pulled her back against his bare chest, and his lips brushed her hair as his arms went around her. "You have to stop, a little bit, being quite so bull-headed."

"You have to stop, a little bit, being quite so bull-headed," she echoed back and turned in his arms, smiling up at him. "It's that red hair of yours," she said ruefully.

"Our children are doomed to it." His fingers groped for the opening to her skirt, finally finding the button in back as his lips nuzzled the soft hollow of her neck. "The boys will end up five-one and the girls six-three. You know that, don't you?" The short zipper came down; the skirt slid easily over her hips. "Do you want children, Loren?"

She found his belt and weaved it slowly through its loops, looking up at him. "No more than five-hundred."

"See? We agree on everything that matters." He stopped undressing her for a kiss, his palms gliding sensually, evocatively, over the mauve lace teddy that clung to her figure. She kissed his shoulders, then his chest, and her arms wound around his neck. Buck teased her ear as if it were the most beautiful part of her body; Loren made a graph of kisses on his chest. They could only tease so long...

When their lips found each other again, they stayed molded together, an urgent hunger in both of them that increased the more they touched. Buck's hands grew more fervent, sweeping up and down the thin silky barrier that separated them, and then again. More slowly, his palms cupped her breasts, lingered at the valley between, then traced down her sides where his palms lingered again. Seductively, his fingers traced a sensual path to her throat, up to her chin, which was suddenly chucked up firmly. Grave dark eyes met hers, and his voice was low. "Loren. How the hell do I get this thing off you?"

She started chuckling. "It's a very common undergarment..." Like a feather, she was tossed on the soft quilted comforter and watched while he took off the rest of his clothes. The moonlight caressed his shoulders and hips, the strange patterns of hair on his chest. He was aroused. The man was built like iron, with a sculpted beauty he would have denied—but then he never saw his body as she did.

His steel yielded to her softness; she had forgotten that in the trauma of the day before. Finally, she believed he needed her as much as she needed him. Just as she believed that in time the last of her ghosts would vanish, that she could yield to his strength and be enriched, not diminished, by it. It was a strange feeling, to give up her old images, to understand that she could be stronger than she was before in trusting Buck, in trusting his love, in opening up emotions that were locked in fear before. Her eyes blurred with sudden, sweet tears.

The next moment he was beside her, his lips against hers, their bodies straining together. The wisp of lace between them created an erotic tension, fanning flames that needed no fanning. Loren cleaved closer to him, needing him just as desperately as he needed her. This night was a marriage, a sealing of commitments and of a bond forged to bridge whatever problems they would have. They would fight through those, live through those, love through those.

He had no difficulty finding the intimate opening to the teddy when it counted. Flesh to flesh felt like a release, like a sudden freedom, like a celebration. He took her then. Temperatures soared; skin took on a fevered flush; the spring night air rushed over silk-dampened bodies. "Buck," Loren cried, and held him deep inside of her. Ecstasy came in a rush with freedom.

So long afterward, the dawn came. They were both exhausted, lying on their sides staring at each other across the same pillow. Buck was still stroking her; she would *not* sleep, did not want to give in to rest. The joy was too great, the future too full to waste even a second of it. Irrationally, she decided she would never again sleep at all.

"Don't ever," he murmured teasingly, "wear that complicated thing again."

"The teddy?"

He nodded. "Whatever you call it."

"I won't, Buck." Tomorrow she was going to buy an even dozen.

WHAT READERS SAY ABOUT
SECOND CHANCE AT LOVE BOOKS

"I can't begin to thank you for the many, many hours of pure bliss I have received from the wonderful SECOND CHANCE [AT LOVE] books. Everyone I talk to lately has admitted their preference for SECOND CHANCE [AT LOVE] over all the other lines."
—S. S., Phoenix, AZ*

"Hurrah for Berkley . . . the butterfly and its wonderful SECOND CHANCE AT LOVE."
—G. B., Mount Prospect, IL*

"Thank you, thank you, thank you—I just had to write to let you know how much I love SECOND CHANCE AT LOVE . . . "
—R. T., Abbeville, LA*

"It's so hard to wait 'til it's time for the next shipment . . . I hope your firm soon considers adding to the line."
—P. D., Easton, PA*

"SECOND CHANCE AT LOVE is fantastic. I have been reading romances for as long as I can remember—and I enjoy SECOND CHANCE [AT LOVE] the best."
—G. M., Quincy, IL*

*Names and addresses available upon request